# A NOBLE BETRAYAL

## BROTHERHOOD OF THE BORDER

### CECELIA MECCA

ALTIORA Press

# CHAPTER
## ONE

K enshire Castle, Northumberland, 1300

Haydn's sword slashed relentlessly.

Over and over he struck his brother's weapon until Hugh finally stepped back and raised both arms. There was a mix of cheers and groans from the men around them in the training yard. Some, no doubt, enjoyed seeing the earl's eldest son defeat his younger brother. Others knew the reason for Hugh's too-quick surrender.

Haydn was out of control. Not making deliberate moves to hone his skills. Instead, he was fighting out of anger. Nay, fury. His brother knew it. Their onlookers knew it. But Haydn didn't care. Rage oozed from every muscle in his body. And if Hugh wouldn't fight him, he would find someone who would.

"He's not in the yard today," Hugh said, apparently discerning his attempt to find their younger brother. "Give it over." He nodded to Haydn's sword. "Come walk with me."

He no more wished to give up his sword than he did to go for a walk. "I'll pass." Haydn sheathed his sword, intending to find a new training partner. But Hugh wasn't having it.

"Either walk with me or I'll tell Mother you nearly took my head off this morning."

"I did no such thing."

Hugh's squire made a face that clearly conveyed his opinion. Haydn ignored him. He had no need for the thoughts of a boy, who'd seen just ten summers.

"I'll tell her you drew blood refusing to wear armour even with unblunted swords."

Their mother hated when they trained "so carelessly" and he was sure to get an earful for such a thing. Lady Sara knew they were warriors. Knew the dangers of not training well. But she also disliked when her sons "acted like fools for the sake of a few cheers." Admittedly, they did have more onlookers when they trained this way.

"There is one problem, brother, with your plan. My sword did not touch you," he said, now irritated with both his current situation and his brother.

"Ahh, but another's did." Hugh raised his shirt. Indeed, an angry new wound stared back at him. Haydn winced. A nasty bugger, and one he should never have incurred in a training yard. His mother would, indeed, be angry.

"I could easily tell Mother the truth. That you attempted to pin your sloppy training, purely for the pleasure of my company."

"Pleasure." Hugh snorted. "If I were looking for pleasurable conversation, you would most certainly not be the one I'd seek."

"And yet, here we are, on the very walk you requested." As boys, they'd often taken this same walk to the castle wall just behind Kenshire's training yard, the one that afforded clear views of the North Sea.

2

"Because you did nearly take my head off back there," his brother said as they climbed the wooden stairs toward the wall walk.

When they reached the top, the closest guard to them nodded in greeting and moved away, leaving alone the two brothers, who looked more like twins than siblings nearly two years apart. Haydn looked out to the sea before giving his attention back to his brother. Looking at him was like looking in the precious bit of mirror their mother kept inside the master bedroom, despite that they were nearly two years apart in age. Hugh's clear blue eyes hinted at the seriousness of the subject at hand.

When Hugh grew serious, it meant trouble brewed. And it did.

"He is a right bastard, Hugh."

"Aye, he is."

"Mother and Father have been loyal subjects their entire lives. How many Kenshire men have lost their lives fighting for him, for his father?" The anger that had dissipated slightly on their walk here returned in full force. When his parents had summoned him to Kenshire from Henham, he'd assumed they wished to question him about his recent visit north. Never could he have imagined the information he'd been about to receive.

Five words that changed his life.

*The king insists you marry.*

And not just any bride, but the daughter of one of King Edward's closest advisors.

His father had handed Haydn a missive. "Apparently rumors of Wallace, and Galien's involvement with him, continue to swirl. A royal courier left just days ago with that."

Reading it, his new reality took hold. With each word he

read, Haydn's hope for a marriage like his parents' was dashed. But more importantly, it also confirmed their suspicions. That his family was in the king's crosshairs. No matter that they'd fought for him many times in the past. His parents' refusal to send men to Falkirk had been the last straw, it seemed, for the king. In the years since, his extended family had admittedly given Edward cause for suspicion. It seemed Kenshire's past support meant little now.

He looked now at Hugh who shrugged. Knowing what his brother was thinking, he said, "Don't."

"Someone needs to say it," his brother responded. "I don't envy your position. But you know it's time. Past time."

Haydn turned back to the sea. It was swirling and angry, dangerous for anyone who misjudged its calm waters from earlier in the day. "If you say so."

"I say so. Mother and Father say so. Everyone knows you have a duty to marry, Haydn. Everyone but you."

An age-old argument, but one it seemed they would revisit. Again. "Neither of our parents are ill. Mother held Kenshire in her own right. She could do so again, if needed. And there are four of us, as well."

"Father will have seen sixty years soon. They will not live forever. Even if you wish it so. And neither will we."

Haydn hated this topic. "It matters not. The king has solved the problem," he said bitterly.

"What will you do?"

Calmer now, courtesy of the training session—and his brother's temperament, even if Haydn would never admit it to him—he resolved not to allow such a rage to overtake him again. The matter was settled. He could resist it all he wanted, but tomorrow he'd leave for London.

"I will bring Lady Phillipa here for the wedding, install her at Hillstone Manor, and return to Rymerden."

His brother blinked. "Hillstone? A bit remote, is it not?" he asked.

After Haydn received his spurs, his parents had given him the small, but beautiful, manor house well south of Kenshire. But it was the castle that Edward gave Haydn's father many years before their falling out, the one the king now threatened to take back, where Haydn resided now. He'd only been to Hillstone on a few occasions. He shrugged. "'Tis safe enough."

"That was not what I meant."

Haydn turned toward the stairs. "I am aware of what you meant. But if you believe for a moment I would take Robert Pernell's daughter to Rymerden, or anywhere where she might spy on our family... The Earl of Sherfield, and by extension his daughter, is not to be trusted."

"I didn't suggest it," his brother clarified. "But have you spoken to Mother about your plan? She will not take kindly to the idea of abandoning your new wife."

Their mother, the countess of Kenshire in her own right before she married Haydn's father, would likely not agree with his plan at all. Fierce but kind, protective as he was, Lady Sara also had a penchant for ensuring the women at Kenshire were treated fairly. But if she had a better plan, he would be keen to hear it.

"Given a choice between a wife I do not know, nor could ever trust, and our family, 'tis not a choice at all." If he included only his parents and siblings as family, they could navigate the king easily enough. But 'twas not so simple. Haydn's Uncle Bryce had married the sister of an influential clan chief. Their intermarriage, and close familial ties with Clan Kerr, were what made them a target of the English king in the first place. Navigating both had proven to be a challenge, but one that his parents and siblings, as well as Haydn's extended family, had accepted. Nothing mattered more than family. Not the king. Not whispers of their being Scottish sympathizers. And certainly not the woman he was being forced to marry.

# CHAPTER
# TWO

*Leedon Castle, Rochester, England*

"Did you hear me, daughter?"

She'd heard him. But Phillipa knew better than to react. She had no wish to see this day, which had held so much promise this morn, grow even worse than it already had with his announcement.

"Aye, Father," she said finally. Back straight, head held high, she uttered the only words he would accept. "If it is your will that I marry the borderer, then it shall be done." Folding her hands together, fingers gripping onto each other to keep them steady, she breathed in, and out. Twice.

*Show him no reaction.*

"We leave in two days' time for Westminster. The marriage agreement has been signed and bans posted."

"May I ask, Father, the sum of my dowry?"

Since she and her sister were mostly worthless in her father's eyes, except for this one thing, Phillipa didn't think he would answer. But he did.

"Three hundred marks," he replied. "And another fifty marks in plates and household items. Your betrothed has promised an estate that you will have the right to during widowhood as dower. More importantly," he leveled a gaze at her that Phillipa knew well, "our liege sees the match as an opportunity to gain insight into the Waryn family's dealings with border clans with which they are allied."

Ahhhh, she understood now. That he gave her so much information, that he was even still speaking with her and had not dismissed her yet, made more sense now. As did the fact that she would marry the Earl of Kenshire's son. Powerful, most assuredly. Landed, she was not certain how extensively. Phillipa knew less of the border lords than she knew of those in the South.

But one thing was certain. If it pleased the king for her to marry this Lord Waryn, as it seemed to, then it pleased her father. Because nothing made him happier than continuing to garner favor with the king and his son. Her father had grown richer, gained more land, in the past twenty years than their family had in three generations.

"Will Lord Waryn permit you to recoup any arrears due from our land until it comes out of wardship?"

She could see she pushed him too far. Her father said nothing as the serving maid took away his trencher. Instead of answering, he waved for the musicians, always on hand in Leedon Hall, to play.

She watched the harpist's fingers move deftly, wondering, as she had so often, how her father could love the sound the instrument made more than she or her sister. Phillipa loved music as much as anyone in the hall. But the way he gazed at the instrument, as he did now, was a look neither of them had received from him before.

Catherine had borne the brunt of his anger for "killing" their mother in childbirth. She was not supposed to have lived, and even Phillipa couldn't shield her younger sister from the truth. He despised her the most, the "cause," or so he claimed, of their mother's death.

Phillipa tried again, this time careful not to reveal her knowledge of "affairs of men," as Father often liked to say. "Can you tell me something of him?"

Annoyed she'd interrupted him as he listened to the lilting notes fill the hall, her father stroked his grey beard, likely contemplating if he would answer her.

"His cousin is Sir Blase Waryn."

That was all he needed to tell her. She'd wondered at the surname and nearly asked if he was related to the famed tourney knight. Phillipa had never seen him but at court the man was already something of a legend despite his young age. She knew precisely three things about him. That he was apparently even more handsome than his father had been. His family had ties to Clan Kerr, some of whom supposedly fought with William Wallace. And the son had won more tournaments at his age than even the father. Sir Neill Waryn's reputation as the greatest tourney knight to ever live having reached her ears even as a child.

"I'd not realized Sir Blase had ties to Kenshire."

Her father's sharp look told Phillipa she said too much. And so she pressed her lips together, waiting for him to respond. He did, finally, many moments later.

"They've grown too powerful," he said.

*For the king's liking.*

He did not need to say the words. Her father did nothing except to please the king. Phillipa was expected to understand her father without being told. And she did.

"You wish me to report anything amiss to you?" she ventured.

For the briefest of moments, her father's keen eyes softened. Not so much that he appeared fatherly. Or kind. Or impressed. But just a twinkling of. . . something. Perhaps she'd pleased him with the question, though it was difficult to discern.

"Aye," he said. "Though it is not just me who wishes it." Turning back toward the musicians, he dismissed her. All that was needed to be said had been, apparently.

*The king wishes me to spy on my husband.*

So Lord Waryn was being forced to marry her by the king, she guessed. Why else would he willingly take a bride such as she? A woman whose father was one of King Edward's closest friends and advisors. Especially if the rumors about his family were true.

Or perhaps 'twas simply a consequence of being inter-married with Clan Kerr and living so close to the border. Often such men, and women, were not trusted simply due to their proximity to the Scots. But other times—more often, in fact—their loyalties did waver, their king and country secondary to their own best interests. Phillipa hoped she was not marrying such a man. One who could so easily disregard his own country.

Of course, her wishes mattered little. She could wish to marry a handsome and honorable man all she wanted. It was never to be her choice. Instead, it seemed, she would be bound forever to this borderer. Her own role in England's devolving relationship with the Scots who terrorized her countrymen would not be greater than she ever could have imagined.

She did not wish to begin a marriage this way, but Phillipa had no choice. Perhaps she could prove to her father she wasn't completely worthless. She just had to sacrifice. . . herself.

# CHAPTER
# THREE

P*alace of Westminster*

"Keep your mouth closed, Holt."

Haydn knew it was directives like that which his younger brother resented. Made him act like the strutting stud he believed himself to be. On a mission to prove to the world, or at least to prove to his older brother and his parents, specifically their father, that he was worthy of their admiration, Holt was equal parts bold and careless.

He could just as easily save the day as turn it disastrous.

But Haydn had little patience for his brother's feelings at the moment. They were about to be presented to the king of England. The one man who could ruin everything their parents had worked so hard to build.

"No promises, brother." Holt side-eyed him; the perpetual smile that usually amused Haydn now served only to annoy him.

"Don't make me regret agreeing to this."

Holt's smile broadened.

Unlike Hugh, who accepted Haydn's decision to come south alone with only a handful of retainers by his side, their youngest brother, three years Haydn's junior, rode into the courtyard at Kenshire like some esteemed tourney knight ready to take on the champion. Attempting to dissuade him would have been useless.

Besides, if he were to have any sword arm by his side, it would be Holt's. Lightning quick, he was a force to be reckoned with. And Haydn should know.

It was Holt who had saved their sister's life.

Haydn reminded his brother of the king's temper on their journey south. Anger him, and they could return to Kenshire without land or title. He'd done as much to other border lords, though King Edward would find deposing an earl more troublesome. Leary of the power of his earls, he also knew firsthand how quickly they could band together against him.

"My lords."

Haydn didn't see the attendant until he stood practically upon them. The tall doors to the hall were open. It was a massive room he'd seen only once before, when accompanying his parents here a year ago for the king's second marriage, to Margaret of France. Struck by the sixty-year difference in their ages, Haydn had wondered if he might be as old when he eventually took a wife. Having rejected every match his parents presented to him, little did Haydn know at the time he'd be returning one year later to take a bride.

Ushered into the hall, Haydn and his brother bowed as they crossed the threshold. As he approached the throne, he was struck, as he'd been every other time in his presence, by the king's size, even seated. Despite his age and one of his eyelids sagging, he was as formidable a sight as he'd been the first time Haydn and his siblings were presented to him as children. Haydn and Holt once again kneeled in front of him.

"You may rise," he commanded in a tone clearly accustomed to ruling men for many, many years. His voice echoed in the massive hall, mostly empty save for a smattering of attendants and two guards. The king stared at him, and then his brother, long enough for most men to become uncomfortable.

But not the sons of the Earl and Countess of Kenshire.

"May I present Sir Haydn Waryn," an attendant announced, "first Baron Waryn of Rymerden Castle, and his brother, Sir Holt Waryn, sons of Sir Geoffrey Waryn, fourth Earl of Kenshire, and Lady Sara, the Countess of Kenshire."

"Your parents tread too fine a line of treason," the king said.

Haydn was not surprised by the king's bluntness, as he was known for such a manner. "They continue to be loyal subjects, Your Grace, as are we. Serving the king and queen of England has been an honor for my family for many years."

"You will recall our grandfather's role," his brother added, "at the Battle of Taillebourg."

Haydn was going to kill him. If the king didn't do it first. Surprisingly, though, Edward's famed temper showed no signs of surfacing. Instead, he leveled Holt a look of clear displeasure.

"Unfortunately, I am unable to recall any Waryn by my side at Falkirk."

He may be the king. His brother may have been rash to speak out. But no one would speak to Holt with that tone.

"You know well, Your Grace," he said, taking the attention away from his brother, "my parents have fought tirelessly for many years to keep the Eastern Marches relatively safe. Your precious resources needed to keep the lawlessness along all other parts of the border are unnecessary courtesy of our men."

"Your men," his eyes narrowed, "and your allegiance to Clan Kerr."

He could not, and would not, deny it. "Their chief and his nephew have achieved something the other Wardens have not. Because of that allegiance, trade flows freely both out of and into England." He paused and then added, "Your Grace."

The target was fully on his back again.

"The same nephew who recently travelled to the French court?"

Dammit. He himself had told Rory not to do so. To be seen so openly with one of the three Guardians of Scotland and ally to the Scottish cause, courted nothing but trouble. Of course, their Scots cousin cared little for the opinion of the English monarch, but Rory should know better. Unfortunately, Haydn and his family had no choice but to care. Incurring the king's wrath had been something they'd somehow avoided until these last few years.

"Our allegiance with my uncle and his father has brought prosperity to a land that would otherwise be fraught with reivers and nothing but trouble for Your Grace."

Never mind more of those reivers were his father's friends than not.

"As I wrote to your father, who should be here now. . ."

Haydn had wondered when the king would mention his absence. It had been Haydn's idea to come alone. To avoid further reminders of their close ties with the Kerrs and Father's reiving friends.

"It is that very allegiance that necessitates you be here.

You will marry the earl of Sherfield's daughter in three days' time here at Westminster."

*Here? In three days?*

Haydn hadn't been expecting that. But his own thoughts mattered little. King Edward had made clear his purpose for this union, not even bothering to hide his motives. The earl's daughter would keep Haydn's family in check.

He did not trust Haydn or his parents.

He may have enjoyed a good relationship with them once. Haydn's father and grandfather may have fought for the Plantagenet kings in the past. But none of that mattered.After Edward's loss at Stirling Bridge, and despite his victory at Falkirk, the king continued to simmer, angry he'd not yet captured the person he held responsible for both. William Wallace was rumored to have travelled to France to gain the king's support, though none knew for certain if it was true. But in his absence, when the king issued a summons asking for feudal service from his magnates across the realm and only two earls, Gloucester and Lincoln, responded to his call, he now had more to blame than Wallace himself for his current predicament, his inability to bring the Scots fully under his control. After the pope demanded Edward withdraw from Scotland, and without the support he'd hoped for, their king had been forced to sign a truce with the Scots.

No one, least of all he and his family, expected the truce to hold. Edward wanted both vengeance against Wallace and to make Scotland the next Wales. Many, including his parents, did not support the king's position and found themselves in an increasingly precarious position. One that would not be alleviated anytime soon.

· · ·

As Haydn was about to acquiesce, to assure the king he would, indeed, marry the spy, his liege surprised him again by lifting his chin and looking toward the back of the hall. Haydn and Holt turned to see the doors being opened again. A man and woman stood there, but they were too far away for him to see either clearly.

"Here is your bride now, Sir Haydn." Edward's tone was cheerier than it had been since he and Holt entered the hall. And why not? The king would continue to enjoy the fruits of his family's border protection while keeping them in check courtesy of the woman who made her way toward them now.

Or so he thought.

# CHAPTER
# FOUR

Having served the late queen as one of her ladies-in-waiting, Phillipa had been in this hall many times. Had been in the presence of the king many times. She knew others were very afraid of him—one man purportedly fell off his horse, dead, in a fright at the sight of the fearsome king—but to her King Edward had always been kind.

Of course, she was not so naive as to think the man was kind by nature because of it. He had done horrific things, and also some that people like her father called visionary and brilliant. No doubt both were true.

"Lady Phillipa." The attendant opened the massive doors after greeting first her father, and then her. She nodded, took a deep breath, and stared straight ahead. Her gaze fell on the men before the king, and though she couldn't see either of them clearly yet, they both stood tall, proud. Dark hair, even darker than her own. They were young men, though that she'd expected. Indeed, Amice had told Phillipa she should be pleased by that fact.

How many noblewomen had they both seen married to

men her father's age, or older? The king himself, for example.

"Cocksure borderers," her father muttered beside her. At least there was no doubt as to his opinion of the northern knights. She'd learned precious little since her father's announcement about these men. The earl and lady of Kenshire had four children, three boys and a girl, all close in age. The eldest, the one she would marry, was a baron in his own right.

Heart hammering as they approached, Phillipa strained to see the men. Both appeared fit, but before their faces came into view clearly, she diverted her attention to the king. He would not take kindly to her staring at her future husband at the expense of ignoring the most important person in the room.

Indeed, she fell onto her knee gracefully before King Edward, her father doing the same. It was only when Edward bade them both to rise that she attempted a peek at her betrothed, but Phillipa's father now stood between them. Instead she kept her eyes trained on her liege.

"Lovely as always, Lady Phillipa."

"You honor me by saying so, Your Grace."

"Robert Pernell, 6th Earl of Sherfield," the attendant announced, "and his daughter, Lady Phillipa."

"Sherfield," the king grunted to her father. "Are you prepared to give your daughter to Lord Waryn?"

Since her father had met with the king last eve, she knew this was nothing more than a formality. A show at which she was invited to appear but not participate. She'd been warned already to say nothing unless directly spoken to, as if she'd not been practically raised at court.

"I am, Your Grace."

"And you," he said to Lord Waryn, "are prepared to accept his daughter three days hence as your wife?"

When her father first told her they'd marry immediately, at court, she'd mourned the loss of time to prepare her wedding. But as Amice—her maid, only four years her senior but already a widow—pointed out, it was just as well to get the deed done.

"Aye, Your Grace."

She had to see him. She had to know if his visage matched the velvety smoothness of that deep voice. At the risk of angering her father by being too bold, she leaned forward and peeked over at the man. Blinking, Phillipa leaned back and pretended to focus on the king as he spoke to both men.

*That* would be her husband?

The man appeared as if he'd been carved by a master sculptor. There was not one feature out of place. If he had walked into the hall during one of the king's elaborate banquets, every woman in the hall would speak his name. Widows, like Amice, would smirk knowingly, leaving virgins, like her, to guess at how a man so handsome could make them feel. Thankfully, Amice had been with her for many years and Phillipa considered her a friend. She'd been by Phillipa's side before, during, and after her marriage. Because of it, Phillipa knew things an innocent should not.

And for the first time in her life, she wanted to know more.

That shameful thought was followed by another.

This was no love match. Of course, few marriages were, but at least her friends had married with the possibility of love, or at least companionship, to hope for. There would be no such hope for their union.

"I leave you to preparations," the king said now, watching her. Was it Phillipa's imagination, or did he seem to be scrutinizing her reaction? Did he guess the direction of her thoughts? Question her loyalty? Phillipa could not allow that. For her sister's sake, she could not let the king see even a moment of weakness. Steeling her gaze and forgetting about what she'd just seen when peeking around her father, Phillipa squared her shoulders and lifted her chin.

When King Edward dismissed them, she found herself walking from the hall with the very man she'd just told herself to avoid looking at. The gentleman at his side had waylaid her father ahead of them, his hands more animated as he spoke than most noblemen allowed. At least here, at court. One of many differences, she supposed, between them and the borderers.

Phillipa peered at her betrothed again. He said nothing, staring ahead as if this was not the first opportunity for a future husband and wife to converse. Up close, he was even more striking. Tall, yet well-built and not at all lanky like that last fop her father had proposed she marry. Not that she would have had a choice, but Phillipa had been glad negotiations with the baron's son fell through.

She wanted to say something to him. But what would she say? As they exited the hall, Phillipa's father turned to her betrothed.

"We have much to discuss," he said in his gruff manner. The only one she'd ever known.

Lord Waryn didn't even glance her way. He didn't introduce her to his companion, a gesture no doubt intended to leave a message. One which she received loud and clear.

*We may be betrothed, but I am neither happy about the fact nor intend to grant you any courtesy because of it.*

When Lord Waryn inclined his head ever so slightly

toward her, Phillipa's heart plummeted at his expression. He hated her. Or hated this situation. Likely both.

Watching them walk away without so much as one of the men offering parting words, Phillipa closed her eyes, not caring the attendants were watching her. Marriage had been her only hope of escaping the utter disregard offered by her father these many years. But this was not to be the escape she'd hoped for.

Phillipa was simply switching one guardian for another.

Albeit a handsome one.

# CHAPTER
# FIVE

"Sign and we're done here."

Lord Sherfield watched him with shrewd eyes. The man was both cunning and ambitious, a dangerous combination. Haydn had spoken at length with his parents about this very contract, and though he hadn't given Sherfield more than he'd been willing to initially, Haydn was also glad the meeting was finally concluded.

Except. . .

"Pardon me, my lord," he said. "I will be but a moment." Standing with enough force for his future father-in-law to startle, Haydn gave his brother a look that told him to stay. Striding toward the door, he swung it open and stepped into the hall. At the door, a guard. Although Haydn wasn't sure what the man guarded. He supposed here, in the king's wing of the East Tower, guards lurked around every corner.

Running a hand through his hair, Haydn walked toward an empty alcove, its velvet-cushioned seat the respite he needed. He sat, thinking about that signature Sherfield was waiting on. How could he give it, sentencing himself and Lady Phillipa to the very opposite of the kind of marriage his parents enjoyed? He'd never deluded himself into allowing himself to care much about what kind of marriage he would have. But this? Bringing what amounted to a spy into his family? They had no chance of a real marriage.

Where was the lady now?

When he first saw her walking toward him in the hall, Haydn thought for certain this was some cruel jest. Surely a woman that beautiful was not the daughter of a man who looked like Lord Sherfield. Certainly he'd not been expecting for his pulse to quicken at the sight of his future bride.

But with each step closer, it had done just that.

She was the opposite of what many considered beautiful, unlike his sister. Haddie's constant quest to remain thin was one he'd often chided. And though Haddie's appearance should be none of his concern, when a maid had advised her to pluck out hairs for a "more desirable forehead," he'd told her the advice was nonsense. Neither did he believe looking as if one had never seen the sun before was advisable, though popular with his sister and her companions.

Of course, Haddie cared little for his opinion.

As to her disposition, Haydn had been raised by a woman who held a castle after her father's death against forces seeking to take Kenshire from her. His aunt Catrina cussed as much as his uncle, and women wearing men's breeches was not an unusual sight at Kenshire Castle.

His bride, it seemed, was timid. Obedient. The kind of woman another man, a lesser man, might covet. But not him. Nor any of his siblings. He and his brothers were different in many ways, but on this, they agreed. The law governing women was unjust. Their voices, unnecessarily silenced. When Haddie married, she would no longer be legally able to sign contracts, bear witnesses in court, or borrow money. If she wished to remain unmarried, as she did now, none of them could blame her.

"Is it done, then?"

He'd been so intent on watching a wall torch, needed even now despite the early hour, the inner corridor affording little light, that Haydn hadn't seen her coming. He stood, towering over her, his body forgetting that she was as much the enemy to his family as the king himself.

"Lady Phillipa," he said, regretting his lack of a greeting earlier. It had gone against his good manners, but Haydn did not want his future bride to get the wrong impression. They would not remain together, and it would be easier for them both to remain distant. "Nay," he replied without offering an explanation.

Her eyes darted toward the door. "Why are you here, and not in there?"

That surprised him. Perhaps he'd misjudged her?

"I must be back inside."

Her thick, well-manicured brows furrowed. "To sign our marriage contract?"

"Aye."

"My father is still in there?"

"Aye."

Clearly she wanted to ask more. Were she Haddie, or his cousin Rylee, she would have. She'd demand to know why he sat alone in this alcove when he should be inside the chamber finalizing the agreement. And he'd have been forced to explain the momentary doubt. The one that he now pushed aside knowing there was nothing to do but sign the marriage agreement.

"If you will pardon me, Lady Phillipa. . ."

Haydn was so surprised by her hand on his arm as he

moved past her that he froze. They stood close enough that he could smell the faint scent of lavender. One he'd never particularly cared for. Until now, apparently.

"My lord, if you would not mind, but a moment."

"A moment," he replied. "Your father is waiting."

"Of course." She dropped her hand. "I wished to say only that. . . well. . ."

Haydn resisted the urge to tell the woman to speak her mind. She would be his wife in name only. Her timidness was of no concern to him.

"If you learned of this union as I did, very recently and without preamble, I just wish to say. . . " She looked him straight in the eyes. "I wish to say that I am sorry."

His heart lurched at her words. When she looked at him, so earnestly and openly, her deep brown eyes imploring some measure of kindness in him, Haydn nearly softened. Told her he was sorry as well. But if the woman was not a conniving sycophant like her father, it would be all the more difficult to leave her at Hillstone Manor.

It was better this way.

"It is but the way of things," he said instead. "Pardon me, my lady."

When she inclined her head, Lady Phillipa's eyes closed briefly, and he noticed her long lashes daintily touching the soft cheeks in deference to him. When her eyes opened again, he caught them, knowing it was past time for him to leave. Haydn was surprised her father hadn't already come looking for him.

He'd been taught, trained, to do better. To make her feel at ease. To take her hand and tell her how lovely she looked, which would have been an easy truth to say. Explain that she would find in him, in his extended family, a tight-knit brotherhood.

He would tell her that, even if he'd not asked for this marriage, he would never resent her for it, knowing how little choice she had in the matter. And instead, like his aunt and uncle who were also forced to marry due to circumstances beyond either of their wills, as many nobles did, they might find compatibility in time. Perhaps, even love.

Instead, he tore his gaze from hers with a shiver that began in his shoulders and settled in his chest as he hurt the lady for the first, but not the last, time. He would say all of that, Haydn thought as he pulled the door to his grim future back open, but he was no liar.

# CHAPTER
# SIX

"I, Sir Haydn Waryn, take thee, Lady Phillipa, to be my wedded wife, to have and to hold from this day forward, for better, for worse, for richer, for poorer, for fairer, for fouler, in sickness and in health, to love and to cherish, till death us depart, according to God's holy ordinance; and thereunto I plight thee my troth."

With as much emotion as he'd shown during their last meeting—the stilted exchange days earlier, just before the contract for this marriage had been signed—her betrothed said the words that would bind them together forever.

With fewer than twenty people their witnesses in the chapel at Westminster Palace, Phillipa repeated the priest's words back to him. And to her husband. Because now, for better or worse as their vows clearly stated, she was a married woman. No longer the ward of her father but of this stranger, one she'd learned much about these past three days.

As they left the chapel, her father approached but halted in front of them suddenly. When she looked at her husband—the very thought of it, she was now a wife—

Phillipa realized the reason for her father's abrupt halt. Lord Waryn's expression.

Forbidding. Unforgiving.

"I would offer my congratulations," her father said, "but you appear less than amicable to them."

Indeed, there was no doubt her husband did not care for her father by the way he looked at the man now. Did his animosity extend to her? It seemed, based on their brief interactions, it did. And to be fair, Phillipa could not blame him.

"We leave immediately." Waryn nodded past him, which was when she spied the brother mounted on a massive destrier, only eclipsed in size and beauty by the one next to it. As she watched the scene unfold, her own Spanish jennet, Lady, was being brought forward by a footman.

Her father's panic was palpable. "Surely you do not mean to miss your own wedding feast?"

She awaited her husband's answer but knew it before he offered a response. Lord Waryn's lips were pursed, his handsome face like a stone carving. No emotion. Precisely what she'd told Amice last eve. The man was more warrior and very little courtier. Just what she'd expected from a borderer.

"The king, I'm told," her husband replied, "has left for Wales."

"He has," her father replied.

In response, Waryn waited, clearly ready to be on his way.

"My belongings," she said, thinking of the trunks she'd meticulously packed. "And my lady's maid." Phillipa had seen Amice during the ceremony, but she was nowhere to be found now.

"She will meet you at Hillstone Manor."

Hillstone Manor. She'd not heard of it, nor did she know if it was Lord Waryn's primary residence. In fact, she knew very little and was becoming increasingly agitated about the fact.

"I can not travel without her," she started, only to be silenced by her own father.

"If your husband has ordered it, you will obey, Phillipa." Though his tone was even, his eyes flashed at her, leaving little doubt as to his temperament. Nothing angered him more than she or her sister speaking out of turn or questioning his decrees.

"Aye, Father," she said.

"Hillstone," her father muttered. He did not seem pleased but neither did he question Waryn further. If it was beyond odd to whisk the bride from the chapel doors to her future home, without so much as a meal or toast, Phillipa would not know. She'd attended weddings before, but none such as this one. Rushed, without preamble or adequate planning, it was as if this morn were nothing more than a regular mass. Except that she wore her best gown, a maroon velvet lined in gold thread. A gown that was the very opposite of one made for travel.

"My gown," she blurted, earning a sharp look from her father. Phillipa clamped her mouth shut.

"What of your gown?" Lord Waryn asked, clearly impatient to be on his way.

"'Tis of no concern."

He looked as if he would turn away at first, but instead her husband sighed. "If you wish to say something, my lady, do so."

She glanced at her father and a memory flooded back to her. She'd been ten and six. Her father sat next to her on the dais and spoke similar words. They'd been speaking of a possible suitor for her after a previous betrothal had fallen apart. When she heard the man's name, Phillipa had spoken without thinking.

"I will not marry an old man," she'd said, moments before her father slapped her so hard across the cheek that the entire hall went silent. The sound reverberated even over his precious musicians.

"You will never question me again in my own hall," he'd said, his tone inviting no argument. Of course, she'd had none. Embarrassed, her cheek on fire, Phillipa bowed her head and hadn't raised it until well after the meal had been served. It had been the first, though certainly not the last, time her father had struck her.

When her husband waited for her response and then finally realized she'd give none, he inclined his head to her father in parting and descended the chapel stairs. With no choice but to follow, Phillipa lifted the hem of her gown on both sides, not wishing to ride in the heavy fabric, and turned to bow to her father. When she did, holding on to a last hope that he might suddenly embrace her, maybe apologize for his harsh treatment and offer some words of regret for her leaving, he gave her the same look as he had the day she left for court.

As if it mattered not to him whether Phillipa stayed or left.

"Goodbye, Father," she said finally, attempting to ignore the lump in her throat. He hated her. Even now that she was of some use to him, would enable him to remain in good standing—or even elevate his standing—with the king, he looked at her as he would a stableboy.

Leaning forward, he whispered into her ear. "You will write to me by the feast day of Saint Martin."

'Twas in just a few short weeks. What could she hope to learn by then? "Aye, Father," she said as he moved away without so much as another word in parting. He joined the others making their way to the hall, and never looked back. Not once. Phillipa knew this because she watched him, waiting.

Phillipa should hate him back. Amice told her so. Friends of hers at court whose fathers treated them similarly, as if they were nothing more than property to be bartered to the highest bidder, said they hated their fathers. And perhaps they did. But she could not do it. Certainly, she didn't like him. But neither did she wish him ill. Phillipa wished no one ill, not even the man who'd just sentenced her to a loveless, miserable marriage.

She could refuse, of course. But then she would have both he and the king he served to answer to. Perhaps that would be better, Phillipa thought as she made her way down the stairs, than to answer to her husband who watched her as if he might take a dagger to her throat while she slept.

Phillipa had so many questions. When had Amice left, and how had he arranged her belongings without her knowledge? She spied a small, familiar trunk atop the pack-horse that must be hers. What was inside? Where was Hill-stone Manor and how long would it take to get there?

Instead of asking any of them, she mounted Lady, displaying at least one of her skills—something she prided herself on, as it was all she had to herself. She sat upright with a confidence she possessed only here, atop her palfrey. Lady's virtues were her own, her flaws, ones Phillipa both understood and commiserated with. She loved the only gift she'd ever received from her father as much, or more, as she loved herself.

So without assistance, despite her gown, Phillipa grabbed Lady's reins, comfortable for the first time that day, never expecting the look of admiration on her husband's face when she glanced his way for guidance. It was a look she should not hope to garner again, but Lord help her, one she could easily come to desire.

# CHAPTER
## SEVEN

"She's not complained once." Holt turned on his mount. "Haydn?"

He resisted the urge to look back. They'd ridden all afternoon, but he'd only been in her presence once, when they'd stopped for her benefit. At his mother's insistence, they'd taken six men along with them. His wife currently rode in the back with two of them. The others were on their way, with the maid and the remainder of his wife's dowry, to Hillstone.

"Why would she complain?"

Holt looked at him as if he were daft. "Perhaps because you plopped the woman on a horse within minutes of your nuptials, denying her even a wedding feast."

Haydn gave his brother a look, but as usual, he didn't back down.

"Aye, she's dangerous. And this is not a real marriage," Holt repeated his words back to him. "But Christ's wounds, brother."

If he was being harsh, it was for them both. What purpose would it serve, becoming acquainted with a woman he had little intention of seeing often after she was settled? If Lady Phillipa planned to report back to her father, and thus the king, on his family's dealings, he would be certain there was nothing to report.

Haydn looked back, and though he could hear them in the distance, around the bend as they made their way through dense forest, the rest of their party was nowhere to be seen.

"I don't think you realize just how dangerous she could be," he said, not for the first time.

Not just because of how she looked when Haydn first approached her at the foot of the chapel steps. Enchanting. Like the calm before a storm. Beautiful and serene, but he knew better. The maid confirmed it. When he'd approached her to ask for the woman to pack his wife a small trunk as well as her own belongings, as they would both be leaving after the ceremony, the young woman had startled. And complied. But not before she muttered something Haydn heartily agreed with.

*"So it begins."*

Aye, he'd wanted to say. And so it did. As usual, his thoughts meandered to the predicament their family had found themselves in these past few years.

"Breac will not be able to mitigate Galien's action," he said. His cousin Breac had only taken over the position as Lord Warden of the Eastern Marches this past summer, and already his biggest problem was reining in his own family members. "At least Uncle Toren was more discreet."

Though the Kerr Clan Chief supported the Scottish cause, Toren did not do so as openly as his son. It was Galien's rumored involvement with Wallace that had attracted the English king's notice, even if he'd never been caught with the outlaw.

"I worry less about Breac than Rory."

Haydn agreed. He'd been headed to Bristol Manor to talk some sense into Rory when he'd been waylaid with the king's plan. The one that earned him a wife. Haydn had been there when his uncle Bryce attempted to dissuade Rory from fighting, against his own king and country, and with his Scottish cousins, in Galloway.

He was brought back to the present, watching the darkening sky. He'd hoped to make it farther north, but it seemed they'd be camping in the elements this eve. Thankfully they travelled along the river, so any flat spot would do. They were on unmarked land now, the road evidence of it. It was unfortunately not paved with stones or even covered with gravel to temper the mud beneath them. Not ideal for travel, and indeed they'd slowed their pace since turning east, but less travelled also meant less trouble.

"Perhaps you can talk some sense into him. I certainly could not."

Holt had been to Bristol recently and apparently had little success convincing Rory to back down. Like his father, Bryce, his cousin very rarely listened to reason. But everything changed with the king's decree for this marriage, and Rory needed to understand they were clearly targets of Edward's wrath. Once he deposited Lady Phillipa, he would head to the border next.

They rode in silence, Haydn looking for a spot to camp, wondering how his wife would receive the news that they'd not reach their destination and would be spending their wedding night in a tent. At least, she would be spending it in a tent he'd brought just for this purpose. Haydn would sleep under the stars, with his men.

Likely she'd accept the fact with an "Aye, my lord," as she had every other turn of events.

"She's a competent rider," his brother said after they slowed to allow a group of pilgrims to pass. On foot, likely on their way to London, they looked as if they'd been travelling for weeks. It was not unusual to see such a group on the road, but their presence did surprise him on this particular, less known route.

"More than competent," he acknowledged. The way she'd handled her mount said much about the lady, and he could not help but be impressed both with her treatment of the animal and the confidence with which she carried herself on the mare.

"She's beautiful too. I hadn't been expecting that."

Haydn had wondered when his brother might comment on the fact. He was surprised it took him so long. His brother's tastes in women were akin to his own. "Aye, she is that."

"Perhaps. . . " Holt cleared his throat. "You should speak to her."

He slowed, spying a clearing in the woods ahead. "About?"

Aye, this was where they would shelter for the evening.

"About your future? Her future? Maybe she will not prove as dangerous as you believe." Holt looked in her direction as Haydn's wife rode with the men toward him.

"And perhaps," he ventured, ignoring his body's response to the woman he had every right to claim, "she will prove more dangerous than either of us realize."

# CHAPTER
# EIGHT

They likely thought her sleeping.

But how could Phillipa possibly sleep? Though the sky was dark, the evening warm for October with the blankets her husband provided keeping her more comfortable than she'd have imagined on a bed of pine needles, this was her wedding night. Which meant Lord Waryn could arrive at any time to claim her.

She knew from Amice it could be a pleasurable experience, or just the opposite. What would marital relations with a man such as Lord Waryn be like? He was large and unforgiving, every movement of his deliberate. But he was also a very attractive man. So much so that, when she looked at him, Phillipa could almost forget for a moment that he had not spoken a word to her all day, beyond their vows.

If she could have imagined her wedding day, never could Phillipa have imagined that she'd be sleeping, for the first time in her life, out of doors. With a borderer who looked more ready for battle than even King Edward, who was known by all as their warrior king. Flipping onto her side, she listened to the men sitting around the fire, speaking softly. One of them, a young knight named Isaac, had spoken to her, at least. Asked her questions of the king and court. She'd responded, glad for the kindness, until they'd stopped for an extremely brief respite earlier in the day. Afterward, Sir Isaac had avoided her, which was when she realized her husband had likely ordered him to do so.

"Will you go to Bristol?"

She strained to hear them, and indeed, it seemed her husband's voice was hushed most of all. If her father thought to receive any information about the Waryn family from her, she was afraid he would be sadly disappointed.

"What of Lady Phillipa?"

This time, desperate to hear the answer, Phillipa scooted from her bedroll toward the tent's flap.

Silence, and then, ". . . to Bristol. . . speak to Rory. . ."

Who, she wondered, was Rory?

Her husband must have lowered his voice then, because she could no longer hear what he was saying. Scooting back, she closed her eyes, pretended this wasn't her wedding night and that she wasn't now married to a man her father and the king expected her to spy on. Phillipa pretended that when she looked at the man her stomach didn't drop to her knees, and instead tried to sleep.

It wasn't working.

"I know you are not sleeping, Lady Phillipa."

How had he entered the tent without her hearing? That troublesome thought was replaced by another. Was he here to claim his wedding night rights? He hadn't spoken to her all day but chose now to do so?

"I am," she countered.

Surely that wasn't a chuckle. Men like Lord Waryn did not chuckle.

"A shame. I thought we could speak about the remainder of our journey."

Phillipa opened her mouth to ask, "Why now?" but closed it. Speaking back to the man who held her life in his hands would not do well at all.

"Lady Phillipa?"

It was the softer tone she responded to. Almost as if he were. . . human. Spinning in her bedroll and taking the blanket he'd provided with her, she turned to see him sitting on the rock in the corner of her very large tent. When the men had pulled the linen canvas from a bag on the packhorse that accompanied them, she'd been surprised to see them set it up around that very rock. Later, she realized it served as a makeshift seat.

If not for the chill in the air and the hard ground, this might not have been an unpleasant accommodation for the evening. A single candle propped on the small trunk that Amice had apparently prepared for her before being whisked away lent a soft glow around them. Her husband, no longer wearing mail and a tunic but a simple linen shirt instead, appeared decidedly less warrior-like.

"Aye, my lord?"

She found herself staring at his jaw. What an odd thing to focus on, but it was perfect. Angled, strong. Similar to his brother's, but because he smiled less, it lent an unforgiving quality that, frankly, terrified her, knowing they were destined to be adversaries.

"You may use my given name," he said, watching her. "I am, after all, your husband."

Sitting up, but pulling the blanket to her chin, Phillipa caught his eyes dart downward. As her gown was now packed in the trunk, she wore a long-sleeved shift.

"You may do the same," she said. The permission to do

so was granted to so few people she was reminded this man was family now.

"Phillipa," he said, as if testing out the name. "We will travel to Hillstone Manor, as you heard me tell your father."

So many thoughts swirled in her brain, but Phillipa remained silent.

"You have nothing to say to that?"

"I have," she hedged, "questions."

He seemed angry at her now, but Phillipa could not fathom what she'd done wrong. Yet.

"Then why do you not ask them?"

Aye, he was most definitely angry.

"You've not given me permission to do so, my lord."

He glared at her.

"Haydn." And then, because she could not resist, "My lord Haydn."

Her husband did not seem to appreciate the jest. She would refrain from such "silliness," as her father called it. Catherine loved when Phillipa said such things, to make her smile. And she loved her sister's smile more than anything in the world. If only her sister were here with her now.

"As I told you at the chapel, if you've a mind to say something, do it. You do not need my permission to speak, Phillipa."

What an odd notion.

"I do not?"

"Nay, you do not."

"My skin reds easily," she warned him. But he did not seem to understand. "My cheek," she said, letting the blanket fall and pointing to her face as if he did not know where her cheek was located.

He was no longer angry but confused. She began to

explain further when he cut her off. "You are worried I might slap you?"

"If I ask a question that displeases you. Aye," she admitted. "You are my husband," she said, as if to explain her reasoning. But he still did not seem to understand.

"Phillipa." He leaned forward, elbows on his knees, brows furrowed. "How often did your father strike you?"

She did not intend to laugh, but the sound escaped her nonetheless. "Pardon my impertinence," she said. "But I do not believe I can count so high. Not," she rushed to explain, "that I've not been taught arithmetic—"

"I will never," he said with more force than she'd heard from him thus far, "ever hit you."

She was sure he would. When she wrote to her father, something she had no choice but to do, and he discovered as much, he would certainly do just that. But Phillipa would endure a thousand slaps if it meant the king's wrath did not turn on her family. Namely, her sister.

"You do not believe me."

She blinked.

"Has a man other than your father ever laid a hand on you?"

"Nay. But none have ever had the right to do so. The law is clear on this, my lor— Haydn. You have the right to chastise me, your servants, your apprentices. . ." He moved so quickly, she did not even have time to be scared. When he reached down and grabbed her wrist, Phillipa knew she'd gone too far.

"Stand up," he said. And so she did. Fairly dragging her to the flap of the tent, Haydn opened it and called to the others. "Have I," he said, gaining their attention, "or any Waryn man ever raised a hand against a woman?"

She could see their expressions clearly courtesy of the

moonlight, and each one of them looked at her husband as if he'd gone mad.

"Of course not," his brother, Sir Holt, answered. "If they did, one of us would run a sword through their gut."

Seemingly satisfied, he let the flap drop to the ground. But her husband did not release her wrist. Though his grip was not tight, it was firm enough to communicate he was not done with the conversation.

"I will never strike you," he repeated. "And if any man dares to do so, including your father, I will kill them."

She thought he jested, for a moment, but Haydn wasn't smiling. In fact, he'd never looked so serious before.

"I just thought. . ." She looked down to where his firm fingers wrapped around her wrist. He let it go immediately. "You have the right."

"Look at me, Phillipa."

She raised her head. Lord, he was a large man, especially standing next to her.

"I will never raise a hand against you. And when I say that you may speak your mind, ask any question you wish, I mean the words."

A flutter of hope was dashed when his eyes narrowed, however. "But know this, Phillipa. I will defend my family vigorously against any threats. Do you understand me?"

She understood him well. "Aye, Haydn. I understand."

His expression said he didn't believe her. Nor should he. Because she would defend her family, or at least Catherine, too. By any means necessary.

Shockingly, he smiled then. The effect of it elicited another, entirely different, kind of flutter within her.

"So there is a fire within you. I'm glad to see it."

With that, he left. Not a word about their wedding night, or any further details about their future. That, she supposed, was her fault, as Phillipa had the opportunity to ask questions but failed to do so.

Tomorrow, she would. If he truly would not get angry at her for doing so, then what did she have to fear by speaking up? Surely not as much as she had to fear by crossing him. Perhaps she'd learn nothing untoward. Nothing to incur the king's wrath?

And maybe it *was* a will-o'-the-wisp she'd seen at the bog they passed earlier. The idea seemed just as likely, and perhaps less dangerous.

# CHAPTER
## NINE

H e expected to have to wake her. Haydn didn't expect her to walk out of the tent just after daybreak looking so fresh and ready for the journey already. Wearing a traveling gown, the one her maid had packed apparently, his wife was just as lovely today. Her hair, as it had been last eve, was no longer properly coiffed but lay in long waves around her shoulders, held back this morning with a simple strip of ribbon. If some might think it odd, a married woman wearing her hair down and uncovered that way, he certainly did not. Especially as he'd denied her the maid she was surely accustomed to having by her side.

He'd planned for them both to accompany him to Hill-stone, but when Amice admitted she was not a competent rider, he had changed his mind. After what had occurred earlier this month in Galloway, he was anxious to get to Bristol Manor to speak to his aunt and uncle, and attempt, as best he could, to get through to his cousin about the dangers now posed to him. They'd been there all along, of course. And Rory was aware of the consequences of his actions. But with luck, Haydn's nuptials would make him realize the precariousness of their situation.

She caught his eye, and Haydn had to fight to temper his anger at her father. He'd known the man was a bastard. Within minutes of meeting him, he despised him. Men like him, ones who cared for titles and standing and power above all else, were the worst sort in his opinion. He'd told his father many times, if the king stripped them of Kenshire, of their holdings, he'd be perfectly content to join his father's "other" family, the reivers his father had run with many, many years ago. Men, and women, with more honor than Lord Sherfield could ever conceive. Aye, they stole from others. Usually the Scots. But they did it to survive, and their code of honor was one he could understand.

This other code, the king's code, he could not. So many died in the king's ongoing battle to retain power over those who clearly wished for freedom from it.

"Good morn, my lord," she said, walking up to him. And then correcting herself, "Haydn."

"Good morn," he replied as the others prepared to leave their temporary shelter. Holt was nowhere to be seen, and the others already had begun to pack up camp. All eve his brother had chipped away at his resolve. Reminding him she'd done nothing yet to warrant Haydn's mistrust. Asking him how he'd wish Haddie to be treated if she were in Lady Phillipa's situation.

"How will speaking to her put us in danger?" his brother had asked as they sat by the fire. Haydn reminded him that his wife had chosen to retreat to her tent moments after they'd eaten, that he'd not ordered her to leave, but

Holt did have a point. Likely she did so because he'd said very little to her all day, and he'd warned the others to do the same.

So he'd given in, made his way to her tent, and regretted it. Keenly aware that it was their wedding night, but having no notion to make her his bride in truth in a tent. And then those revelations about her father. Something in him had snapped, and now Haydn didn't know if he could put it back together. Still uneasy to reveal too much to her, knowing as he let his guard down he may say something, even inadvertently, that could be used against his family, he nevertheless decided today would be different. There was a fire there, as he'd told her, and Haydn felt challenged now to see if he couldn't bring it out. Let it burn. It could serve her well at Hillstone Manor.

"Did you sleep well?" It had been regrettable that they'd not made it to the abbey, as he'd planned. Haydn was sure sleeping on the ground was a new experience for her, and though he had no plans for this marriage to be anything but one in name only, he also had not intended to be cruel, as Holt accused him of last eve. Though his haste to get away from her father had been justified, as it turned out.

"Better than I'd have expected. Thank you." She nodded to the tent being dismantled by Isaac and Hamon now. "'Tis hard to believe one packhorse carried a tent so large."

He approached her as if she were a deer, cautiously so as not to spook her. "I would apologize, Phillipa, for my treatment of you on our wedding day."

As always, her gaze was measured. "It certainly was not what I'd expected, but then, neither was our marriage," she said. "Much has changed suddenly for me. And for you, I would imagine."

Temporarily, aye. She wanted to ask him something, and though he was in a hurry to be on the road, Haydn wished more for her to ask her questions. He would, if nothing else, ensure she knew no man in his employ while at Hillside would dare mistreat her.

"Go ahead," he prompted. "Ask."

She squared her shoulders, as if preparing for battle. A niggling of sorrow, and another of anger at her father, settled into him. Burrowed, as if uninvited.

"Why did we leave with such haste?"

Holt arrived back at camp. When he began to walk toward them, Haydn shook his head.

"I dislike being at court. If we stayed for the feast, it would have extended our time there for at least a day. As it was, we did not make it to the abbey of St. John's for the night. I'd not intended," he waved his hand, "for this." And also, he needed to get to Bristol immediately. But that, of course, he did not say.

"Why could Amice not travel with me?"

"She admitted you are a much more competent rider and she would have slowed us down."

"Why did you not speak to me about it? Or about anything, in fact."

Phillipa became more and more emboldened with each question that she asked, and he answered without pause. Though this was a trickier one. Some measure of truth was necessary.

"You are the daughter of one of the king's closest advisors. I am a man in the king's crosshairs."

She frowned. "So your solution for this is to simply avoid me?"

"Aye," he admitted.

"Then this will not be a marriage in truth."

No answer seemed preferable to providing one.

"That answers another question," she muttered, turning away from him to watch the men finish preparing to leave. He waited, but she did not ask.

"Which is?" Haydn prompted. When she met his eyes, Haydn was forced to confront the sadness in them. What would everyone have him do? Bring her to Bristol to witness his cousin's treason firsthand? Perhaps a trip across the border to Highgate End where she might even come in contact with Wallace himself? Wouldn't Edward be happy to hear the most hunted man in Scotland was precisely where he thought him to be, hiding out in the lowlands where he continued to train men to fight for Scotland's freedom.

"Why we did not have a wedding night."

He could tell it took every measure of her courage to make the statement. Even attempting to be bold, the flush of pink on her cheeks gave her away. Haydn imagined himself claiming those full lips, pressing himself into her, showing her everything, making Phillipa his in truth. He cleared his throat, offering the full truth this time.

"I'd not have a wedding night in a tent among my men."

She waited.

"We leave for the Cony Inn," he said, "if there are no other questions."

There was one. He could see it in her eyes. But this one, his wife would not ask. So he emboldened her even further, stepping forward. They needed a wedding night if he was to produce an heir, and Haydn could not discern any reason why they should not enjoy it.

Standing so close he could smell her perfume, Haydn leaned down to whisper the answer to her unasked question into Phillipa's ear. "Aye, if we reach the inn before dark." He pulled back, his nose tickled by her hair. She stared at him, wide-eyed, confirming that had, indeed, been her question.

But in taunting her, he'd served only to ensure today's ride would be a long and torturous one for himself.

# CHAPTER
# TEN

The day had been long and grueling. Phillipa had always found solace in riding and was good at it. When she'd served the queen at court, it had been the thing she'd missed most. Short rides and hunting were not the same as allowing herself to roam the countryside without escort, as long as she remained on Sherfield land.

But this was an entirely different kind of riding. Relentless, even. There was no doubt her husband was in a hurry, but why? He'd explained their hasty retreat from court after the ceremony, and Phillipa could not genuinely say she was upset by it. Freedom from her father's judgmental, or worse, nonexistent gaze was something she'd always dreamed of, even knowing it would come at a price. That she'd be handed from one keeper to another.

Haydn's actions since then spoke of another purpose altogether, and she'd begun that day determined to learn what it was. The men spoke, if not always to her, around her. A whispered word here or there. When they'd stopped midday, Haydn and Holt both talked to her briefly. Nothing of significance; they'd simply asked her questions about her time at court, and she answered. In turn, she inquired about their upbringing at Kenshire, admitting that she'd heard of their family, of Blase Waryn especially, but did not know much about them.

Throughout it all, one name kept creeping up, and she thought perhaps it might be the reason for their haste. Rory. And so when Haydn told her he had another brother, and sister, neither of whom were named Rory, she was surprised—she'd been certain it must be one of his siblings.

Their party rode now into what appeared to be a very small village, her husband's words coming back to her as they had all day. *"Aye, if we reach the inn before dark."*

"What is this place?" she asked Haydn, who rode next to her.

"Fenwall St. Eastake," he replied as the others rode ahead of them.

"What an odd name." She spied no more than twenty homes. A windmill. And as they drew closer to the center, a well around which ten or so people milled. No church manor home or church even. "That is the inn you mentioned?" Phillipa asked. As they rode past the well, the townspeople watched them with a combination of fascination and suspicion.

"Aye." Though he spoke more today than the day before, Haydn still said very little. And not only to her, she'd noticed, but the others as well. Guarded, though for her benefit or not, Phillipa was not sure.

"It appears we've not reached it by dark," she said. Haydn had just dismounted, so she could not see his face. When he handed the reins to Isaac and turned toward her, Phillipa was surprised to see him smiling.

Though she could dismount easily enough on her own, when Haydn reached up for her, Phillipa found her hand grasping his. It was as firm a grip as she expected. When her feet reached the ground, he did not let go. Instead, Haydn pulled her toward him.

"You misunderstood my meaning," he said, his voice low. "But I think you know that already. Though I admire your audacity in trying."

She was beginning to learn that about him. Saying what she was thinking seemed to please him. The very opposite of her father or the king. She would test her theory.

"Audacious would have been feigning an inability to continue when we stopped by the stream earlier." The thought had occurred to her.

At first she thought he let her hand go finally because she'd dared too much. But his smile stayed in place. "So you've been thinking about the matter, have you?"

She could lie, but there would be enough of that in their marriage. The truth, when possible, was always preferable. "Aye."

Something happened with his smile then. It turned. . . sly. "I believe you will be pleasantly surprised, Phillipa. There is naught to be apprehensive about."

With each response he did not take offense to, she felt more and more emboldened. "Says a man who's likely had much experience with. . ." She really should have thought out her words more carefully. "Relations," she finished.

"Relations." He gave Lady's reins to Holt, who'd approached them.

"Will you be staying here for the eve or coming inside?" his brother teased them.

They looked so much alike but, she began to realize, the two men were very different. Haydn's smile came easier today than the day before, but Holt's never seemed to disappear. Her husband didn't answer his brother, so Holt rolled his eyes and led the horse around the inn's entrance to, she assumed, a stable.

"I am sorry if you worried about this," Haydn said when his brother walked away.

The apology was so unexpected, she was unsure how to respond at first. "I was told," she began, and then clamped her mouth shut. His easier-than-expected manner was doing things to her. Imagine, what she'd been about to blurt! 'Twas not something she would say aloud to anyone, save Amice.

"What were you told?" he prompted.

She shook her head. Nay, she would not repeat it.

Haydn frowned, his eyes boring into hers as he waited.

She shook her head again.

"Phillipa. Did we not discuss this very thing last eve? If you have something you wish to say, do so."

"I have nothing to say," she assured him. Still, he didn't move. "'Tis not the same at all. This matter is delicate. Last eve we discussed my fear of angering you."

"Which I've dissuaded you from, I hope."

She thought about how to phrase this. "I do not believe you will be angered if I speak my mind on this. But 'tis not a topic that should be spoken of aloud."

He was definitely not pleased with her answer. "I am your husband."

"But a stranger to me."

"Then we shall rectify the matter. Come." He nodded toward the inn. "Ask your questions, but know this. Before the end of this night, you will tell me what you've been told about making love."

Phillipa's hand flew to her chest.

Haydn chuckled. "I would apologize for my bluntness, but it seems that is precisely what you need, my dear wife."

He crooked his arm such that Phillipa immediately took it, as if they were walking not into a timber-framed two-story building but the great hall of an English noble. It was the first time since they exchanged vows that she actually felt as if she were married.

Well, Phillipa would feel well and truly married this eve, and if she were being honest with herself, she was in equal parts worried and curious.

Her wedding night, for better or worse, had finally arrived.

# CHAPTER
# ELEVEN

B y the time they'd finished their meals—meat pies and freshly baked bread—Haydn could not stop staring at his wife. Was she truly the same woman who had stood in front of that chapel and said not a word?

They sat at a table tucked into the corner. Their host, the innkeeper of the Cony Inn, kept their mugs filled all eve. The first time Haydn had come here with his father on the way to London, the innkeeper had already been elderly.

Haydn's attention turned to his wife, who sat across from him, next to Holt. Every moment that passed, she seemed more and more comfortable offering her opinion. At first she'd glanced at him each time someone asked her a question. A fact that made him seriously consider heading back to London to throttle that father of hers.

They all knew not to breathe a word of anything relating to the Waryns or Kerrs. Instead, they spoke of politics. Of travel. He learned of Phillipa's sister, of whom she seemed quite protective. And of her time at court serving the queen.

When Hamon asked her how a woman such as she was

not already married, she said, "A broken betrothal. A queen who forbade her ladies to marry while they served her." Phillipa turned more serious. "A father so beholden to the king that he'd not make a decision without his approval." As if realizing she'd said too much, or had been too candid, his wife had lifted a mug of ale to her lips, drinking more deeply than she'd done since they arrived.

Even now, as he watched her interact with Holt and his men, Haydn wondered if the tone of her response had meant what he thought it had. The comment was certainly not one of reverence for her father, or the king. He'd assumed her full loyalty would be to both, but now Haydn wondered if perhaps that assumption was misplaced. Between what she'd told him of her father, and now this...

"How far north have you been, my lady?" Hamon asked her.

Hamon, the son of a baron and neighbor to Kenshire, had only earned his spurs the year before. Though his sword was well-honed, Hamon had much to learn still. Though the question was a good one.

"I'm afraid this is the farthest north of London I've been," she said. "My home is just north of Glastonbury. My mother was co-heir with her younger brother with property in Nottinghamshire and Yorkshire. But I've not been there myself."

"Your mother," he prompted. It was the first time she made mention of her.

"Died in childbirth when Catherine was born." She shrugged. "Denying my father the son he so desperately hoped for."

The bitterness in those words told him more than the words themselves. So her father blamed Phillipa and her sister for his lack of sons. Which accounted for his mistreatment of them, for if he abused Phillipa, surely he did the same to her younger sister.

"My aunt Emma and her husband have three daughters," he said, hoping to further demonstrate the difference between he and Phillipa's father. "My uncle dotes on them all, as your father should have done, rather than blaming you for something that was not your control."

His guess hit its mark; Haydn could tell from her expression.

"Dotes. My father does not know the meaning of the word."

It was her lack of emotion that made him want to comfort her. Which, of course, he could not, and would not, do. He'd promised himself at the start of this journey that he'd speak as little as possible, consummate their marriage as was his duty, ensure she was well-installed at Hillside, and move on.

Feeling pity for her would not do. He had to change the tone of the discussion. Haydn raised his mug. "To the border. You are one of us now." He'd meant only that she would be leaving the stifled sophistication of the South for the less nepotistic and more independent North. But, Haydn realized belatedly as they drank, it sounded like much more.

Indeed, she caught his eye and looked at him with a measure of longing that had nothing to do with the upcoming evening. And he wasn't sure which was worse. If Haydn had hoped to keep a distance between him and his wife, he was failing miserably.

"My father," she said hesitantly, "says the borders are more dangerous now than ever. Is it difficult, living so close to the unrest?"

The question, asked innocently enough, was too close

to home for him. Of course, Hamon took it upon himself to answer.

"Not as dangerous as it will be if this truce does not hold."

Holt, for all his talk of offering more kindness to his wife, eyed his wife with a suspicion likely only Haydn could discern. "Do you believe it will hold?"

All three men waited for his wife's response.

"I. . ." she blinked. "I am not privy to discussions that would give me cause to believe aye or nay."

If his mother, or Haddie, or most of the women in his family were to say such a thing, Haydn would roar with laughter. But from his wife? The statement might be true. Or not. Either way, she'd offer them little insight into the mind of the king.

"Your father is King Edward's closest advisor, is he not?" Holt asked the question with a tone so light if it had wings, the words would fly through the air.

"One of them," she said, swallowing hard. Clearly uncomfortable. "But he tells me little." Phillipa caught Haydn's eye. She wanted him to rescue her, and dammit if Haydn didn't do just that.

"A fact I can attest to," he said, gaining a raised eyebrow from his brother, "having met the man."

The look of gratitude she gave him made Haydn wish he could take back the words.

"This is no way to spend your wedding night," a loud voice burst into their discussion from behind him. One that hardly matched the frail man who came into view.

Haydn tried to stand but Big Barney, as he was known, laid a hand on his shoulder.

"No need, m'boy." Barney looked at Haydn's wife. She was very much out of place here. He was aware of the fact, and indeed Phillipa should be staying in a manor house, at least. Tomorrow, if they reached it, they would be guests of another friend of his father. But in the meantime, in his haste to reach Bristol Manor, they would do what was necessary.

"This is Big Barney, owner of the Cony Inn and an old friend of my father's," he told the group. "I am pleased to introduce you to two of my men, Sir Isaac and Sir Hamon, and my wife, Lady Phillipa. You know Holt, of course." His brother had spoken to Big Barney when they'd first arrived.

Fairly leaning on the back of Haydn's old wooden chair, Barney nodded to each of them but held his wife's gaze. "Apologies for not greeting you sooner. My favorite goat got loose. Had a bit of a time catching her."

The thought of Big Barney, certainly not as able as he'd once been, chasing a goat made Haydn smile. Holt must have been thinking the same.

"You chased her down yourself?" his brother asked.

"O' course not, boy. Do I look like I can chase anything these days?" No one answered. "But there was a time I could catch anything. Or anyone. Reiver," he said to Phillipa. "And not ashamed of it. Did what needed to be done."

Phillipa smiled. "As do we all, Master Barney."

"Ha," he cackled. "Ain't that right?" He pointed a crooked finger at Haydn. "Their father ran with me, and the moonlight o' course, for a time."

"Your father," she asked Haydn, "was a border reiver?"

He never got to answer.

"Damn good one too. When those damn Kerrs took Bristol and left 'em without a home, the Waryns did what they needed to survive. As we all do, like you said, my lady. And look at 'em now. An earl. Owners of Bristol Manor once again. And they call Clan Kerr family now." Big Barney shook his head. "A turn o' events I never saw comin'."

Haydn could do without the family revelations. Not that he was ashamed of his father for reiving, of course. His youngest brother Hugh tangled himself with his father's old friends from time to time, much to their mother's dismay. But the less Phillipa knew, the better. Especially about his extended Scots family.

"As you said, Big Barney, this is our wedding night," he interrupted the trip down memory lane. "Of sorts."

Barney smirked knowingly. "Best room in the inn waitin' on you, Lord Waryn."

Now he was Lord Waryn when a minute ago he was "my boy." If he'd learned anything of his father's reiver friends, it was that unpredictability should always be expected. Barney stood back to let he and Phillipa rise. When they did, he took Haydn's place, evidently prepared to tell more stories to those remaining. Lifting a ring with one key hanging from it, Barney handed it to him. "Two doors from the room you stayed in when you were here last. End of the hall, on your left."

"Barney, it's been three years since I've been here last. You must have hundreds of travellers here a year. How do you remember my room?"

The old man winked at him. "Same as you remember how to wield that fancy sword at your side, my boy. It is my job, as surely as yours is to protect that beautiful wife of yours."

To protect Phillipa. If only he could do that while protecting his family too.

Ignoring the taunts they received from their companions, Haydn led Phillipa from the hall. All eve she had looked at him with a mixture of curiosity and apprehension, and though he still did not intend for them to become close on their journey, he could ensure her first experience would be pleasurable.

"So, my lady wife, are you ready to tell me what you were told about this eve so I can determine whether I need to live up to, or debunk, your idea of what lovemaking entails?"

Halfway up the stairs she turned back to look at him. Haydn had not been expecting her to appear so relaxed. The ale, thankfully, had taken its effect.

"I've been told this could be the worst, or best, evening of my life."

"A fair assessment, actually," he said. "And I can easily assure you, it will be the latter."

# CHAPTER
# TWELVE

Phillipa opened her eyes, attempting to discern her surroundings. It was dark, still. And she was in bed. Sitting up, she glanced around the room. A candle burned, her bed empty. Memories of last eve flooded back. She remembered arriving in the room, unsure how to undress with her husband looming next to her. He left so she might "feel more at ease," and so she quickly stripped down to her shift, washed herself with the bowl of water and cloth left for them, and then lay down in the bed.

That was all she remembered.

A pain in her temple reminded her of the ale she'd drunk, certainly more than she was accustomed to consuming. But tankard after tankard had been brought to their table, and Phillipa found herself enjoying the simple meal with Haydn and his men. It was as if, for but a moment, they were not on opposite sides of a conflict that had no signs of abating, despite the pope's insistence that the king make peace with Scotland.

The door opened abruptly, and Phillipa's next question was answered. Haydn was fully dressed and ready for the road. It was, indeed, morning. Though before sunrise, otherwise she might see light peeking through the wooden shutters.

"'Tis time to leave," he said, closing the door behind him. "The men and horses are ready."

"Why did you not wake me sooner?" she asked, rubbing her temple.

"You slept so soundly," he said, sitting on the edge of the bed. "I will ask the maid belowstairs if she has garlic readily available for your head. Too much ale does not agree with you?"

"Apparently it does not. I've not had cause to learn of the fact before last eve."

Her husband appeared much as he had the night before. Guarded, but more relaxed. Handsome, but never leering. Even as his gaze dipped to her breasts outlined beneath the linen shift, it was so different from the looks she received at court. Those made her feel as if she were about to be devoured. Haydn's was more. . . deferential. But his eyes, when he raised them, were anything but.

They were filled with desire. And her body responded accordingly. Phillipa's core clenched, and despite the throbbing in her head, her pulse began to race. Would he claim her now or nay as the men were prepared to leave?

"I fell asleep."

"Aye, you did."

"My apologies. I meant no insult to you, Haydn."

"Apologies? For being exhausted?" He sighed. "It is I who should apologize. Our pace has been brutal, and I'm sorry for it."

"You are anxious to get home?"

He didn't answer immediately. Phillipa could tell he was guarding his next words.

"I need to get back up north, aye," was all he said. "But tonight you shall sleep in a real bed. We should make Brookhurst Manor by nightfall."

Their eyes locked.

"And then?" she asked.

"And then I will introduce you to a dear friend of my uncle's."

"Your family has many friends scattered about England, it seems."

And Scotland too, but he'd not point that out to her.

"I've a large family," he acknowledged. She waited for him to expand on that, "My mother was an only child but my father has two brothers, Bryce and Neill, and a sister, Emma. We visit an old friend of Emma's husband.

"I've heard of Sir Neill Waryn."

"Of course. Everyone has heard of my uncle Neill."

"And his son, Sir Blase."

"My cousin is an even more skilled tourney player than his father, aye." He paused. "We've discussed this before, Phillipa. If you wish to ask me something, there is no need to hold back."

"Your Uncle Bryce. He is the one who lives at the border?"

She was surprised he revealed so much. "You are hesitant to answer."

"I am," he admitted, looking at her as if he found her enticing. As if maybe he'd been disappointed she'd fallen asleep before he returned to the room last eve. "Should I be?"

She pulled the coverlet to her chin, aware her answer was too delayed. "We find ourselves in an unfortunate position as husband and wife," she said finally. "Do we not?" It was not something she'd have said to him three days ago. She found it easier and easier to be honest with him.

"Do you know why the king facilitated our marriage?"

"Your family is a powerful one," she hedged. "And he wished to reward mine for its service."

"Perhaps." He did not seem angered that she avoided the question.Haydn stood. "And because he does not trust you," she added. "Or your parents, more like."

"Because?"

"Because of your connection to Clan Kerr. Your aunt, is it not?"

He seemed surprised she knew of the connection. "My father's brother Bryce married the clan chief's sister, Lady Catrina. They were enemies," he said, "for many years. Bristol Manor had once belonged to my family, but as with many properties along the border, it changed hands, into the Kerrs'. When my father and Uncle Bryce took it back. . ." He hesitated with the next part of the story but continued."The chief's sister was caught in the crosshairs. Taken captive. By my uncle Bryce."

She must have looked horrified, but Haydn laughed. "That was many years ago. And not long before they fell in love and married. No need to worry for my aunt Catrina. She is tougher than any man I know. Raised among brothers, she cusses more than all of them combined. And gave my uncle Bryce a time of it, from what I understand."

"And now. . ."

"And now she and her family are our family. My cousins are like siblings. We call her three brothers 'uncle' and their children 'cousin' even though 'tis through marriage. Once enemies, our family and the Kerrs are now allies strengthened by blood." He stopped there. It seemed that was all he would say on the matter.

"You will protect them, including your Scots relatives, above all."

He did not need to answer her. The truth of her words resonated in their very presence here, in this inn. Hayden stood.

"Then you understand how I feel about my sister. She is ten and six, and I was her closest companion."

Did he notice she mentioned only her sister. Not her father, or her king, or country. It was not unusual for a borderer to be more loyal to his family or clan than country, from what she understood. But a southerner, like Phillipa? A woman who'd been raised at court? Especially given her father's relationship to the king? Surely he understood the implications of those she'd omitted.

"And you would protect her above all others," he said, resigned. "Tell me, Phillipa, have you been instructed to spy on me and my family?"

# CHAPTER
# THIRTEEN

A s the manor house came into view, Phillipa could not stop her hands from shaking, as they'd done since the attack. They'd been riding along when suddenly Haydn was beside her, yelling for Isaac to to stay with her. The look in his face was one she'd never forget. He'd hardly looked at her, but the anger and resignation, as if he knew what was about to happen, was palatable.

"Come my lady," Isaac had said as the others rode ahead. Lady danced relentlessly under her, wanting to flee. Issac had dismounted and come to her, claiming Phillippa's mount. Then leading them both from the path, they made their way slowly forward. That's when she had heard the first shouts. Closer and closer then inched ahead, a scream piercing her ears as she exchanged glances with her companion.

"WE SHOULD REMAIN HERE," he'd say, clearly wanting to do anything but. Phillippa urged Lady on anyway. She had to know what was happening. Her husband was clearly in danger. But when they finally reached the clearing, the clanging of swords ringing in her ears still, it was difficult to discern what, precisely, was happening. Phillippa spotted Hadyn, and her chest had constricted as his sword whipped to and fro, his opponent unrelenting. She'd seen the bodies then, three of them. Holt stood over one of them just as she'd noticed the blood on his sword.

Isaac had moved in front of her, so she had to peer around him to see. By the time Phillippa had regained her bearings again, men were running away, mounting as quickly as she'd ever seen men do so before. That's when Haydn looked toward her, his eyes, for a brief moment, seemingly to convey relief.

An attack. Her husband and his men were all alive, but there were, she noticed then, three men at their feet. Phillipa had known fear before, but not like today. Never like today.

Many times, especially when she'd first begun to serve the queen, she had been worried. That she would make a mistake. Displease her mistress. Or her husband. She'd worried how her father would react. Whether it was a broken betrothal, even if her intended had done the break-ing, or a marriage prospect coming to visit, Phillipa always worried how he would respond.

When her father and the king disagreed after hearing Balliol and Bruce's arbitrators—her father having been responsible for poring through documents concerning each man's claim to the title of King of Scotland—and had backed Bruce's claim, she'd not been as scared as she'd been today. On edge since the morning, when Haydn asked if she was spying on him, Phillipa had retreated from saying too much. Asking the wrong question. Silent all morn, and into the afternoon when they'd been forced to cross a stream that, in her opinion, should have been bridged, she had been reluctant to join the conversations around her.

As usual, they spoke of nothing of significance, because of her presence, no doubt. The weather. How they might best navigate the landscape. Comments on the pilgrims they'd passed.

And then, the attack.

"Beautiful, is it not?" Hamon asked her, startling Phillipa out of her reverie. His thick beard and heavy accent made it more difficult for her to read his lips as he rode up to her. Phillipa had barely made out the words.

"Aye," she said as he reached her. Apparently they'd skirted the village but Phillipa could see it now from this vantage point as they climbed the hill toward their temporary lodgings. Despite the incident, they had made good time and the sun had not quite set. "Why is it called Brookhurst Manor? It seems larger than many castles, to me."

"'Tis not the size that matters, my lady. But the defenses. Its lack of real fortifications make it a manor house."

"I would disagree," Holt said, appearing from nowhere on Hamon's other side. "Size can matter at times."

"You say that because your family is well-endowed." He looked to her. "Kenshire Castle, I mean," Hamon clarified.

When the two men chuckled, Phillipa felt as if there were some sort of jest she did not understand. Any further questions would have to wait, however, as they passed through the gate. Indeed, she understood the difference now. There was just one inner bailey and the entrance to the keep, mostly unprotected. Though the courtyard was large, that just one gatehouse separated would-be attackers was something she'd never seen before. Her own home, though similar in size to Brookhurst, was much better defended.

"It's never been attacked," Hamon said as she stared at the keep in awe. "If Brookhurst were located at the border, its lord would not enjoy such a peaceful existence."

He said no more as a man, nearly as tall as her husband, approached them. Clearly this was the lord of the manor. Though he dressed simply, walking from what appeared to be the stables, it was the way he carried himself that gave away his identity.

"Haydn," he bellowed to her husband who'd been riding ahead of them since the attack. "Welcome to Brookhurst."

Haydn dismounted as the two men greeted each other warmly. By the time the rest of their party joined them, she'd missed part of their conversation. Looking around and seeing few people milling about, Phillipa wondered if it might be supper. Or mass. She could not tell the time of day for certain.

"You've arrived at the right time. Supper is served just now."

"Do you not eat?" Haydn asked as their horses were taken from them.

"My wife's beloved mare is ill," he said, nodding to the stable. "Speaking of my wife, she will be pleased to have another woman to sup with this eve."

Phillipa inched closer toward the men.

"May I present my wife, Lady Phillipa."

Their host clearly had not been expecting that. "Wife? I thought perhaps you Waryn men might never give your poor mother a grandchild."

He was similar in age to her father, a handsome man, and quite jovial, not unlike Holt.

"Lady Phillipa is the Earl of Sherfield's daughter," her husband added.

Lord Brookhurst's smile fled from his face quicker than a rabbit running from an arrow. Bowing slightly to her, their host stood straight again, clearly confused. Holt intervened.

"They were gently nudged to marry by the king."

"Ha!" Lord Brookhurst quickly regained his humor. "Gently nudged. I know no Waryn man to be gently nudged toward anything. More like clobbered over the head with the threat of our esteemed king taking Kenshire away, no doubt?"

He'd guessed the truth of it quickly enough.

"We were attacked, near the Cuald's Combe. Soldiers who haven't quite made their way home from Annandale."

"Cuald's Combe is south of the land we claim, but an old, well-maintained road makes it well-travelled," Lord Brookhurst acknowledged. "Are any of them still alive to bring the tale home?"

That he seemed unconcerned about the most terrifying afternoon of her life, and so confident that Haydn and his men vanquished the attackers, might have been a surprise to her. But it wasn't. Not after seeing Haydn and Holt fight.

By the time she and Isaac had arrived on the scene, Phillipa had no idea how it began or even what was happening. Her companion had leaped from his mount, grabbing Lady's reins. Her horse had not been trained for battle and attempted to flee, but she and Isaac together managed to stay her as the incessant clanging continued.

Try as she might, she could barely keep track of who was whom, and knew only by the time Haydn rode away from the fray, there at least three men dead and another three that had fled in the direction they'd just travelled from. For so long she'd heard of battles, and indeed saw men train with regularity, and had even attended tourneys before. . . but this had been different. Unlike any of those other instances. Oddly, she'd been worried more for the men— for Haydn— than for herself. But the thought that death was not some far-off idea but staring her in the face. . . Phillipa shuddered.

His and his brother's swords were both covered in blood. Hamon was gone, later explaining how he chased the attackers long enough for them to believe they were being hunted down, ensuring they'd not return.

"Unfortunately, half of them fled," Haydn said. "But a meal and hot bath for ourselves and my wife would be greatly appreciated, my friend."

"Both are yours." Lord Brookhurst clapped Haydn on the back. "And then you can explain how you've managed to incur King Edward's notice again. And tell me of your uncle. I've not seen him for nearly a year. It's been much too long. Come."

They were led directly into the hall where supper was, indeed, already underway. A handsome woman similar in age to their host sat on the dais. And though her hair was pulled atop her head, auburn curls escaped everywhere. Led to the corner of the dais where a bowl of scented water lay on top of a wooden stand, one by one they washed their hands and climbed the wooden steps to join her.

The lady of the manor stood.

"Apologies for coming into your hall as such," Phillipa said.

But Brookhurst stopped her. "Lady Phillipa is the earl of Sherfield's daughter and Haydn's wife. They made their way north from London, and their party was attacked on the road."

The hostess bowed, Phillipa's station demanding it. "Please do sit, my lady. Lord Waryn and Sir Holt, join us."

Isaac and Hamon sat below them at a trestle table with the other men of Brookhurst. And just now, Phillipa wished she could join them. Here, all eyes were on her, and she had to pretend all was well when nothing was further from the truth.

She complimented the hall and the food. Answered Lady Kristine's questions and ate quietly, making it through most of the meal. And mostly avoided the man sitting next to her until their fingers brushed as they reached for the same apricot tart that had been served on a pewter tray between them.

Until now he'd spoken mostly to his brother on the other side of him, but her husband looked at her when they touched. And had yet to look away.

"Are you well?" he asked, likely for the tenth time since the attack.

"Aye." She pulled the tart toward her and took a bite. Delicious. Phillipa loved sweets above all.

"You've not witnessed a battle before."

"Nay," she admitted. "I have not."

He frowned. "It is different than a tourney," he said, echoing her thoughts. Phillipa had often witnessed the clashing of swords and violent smashing of a wooden lance off a shield. But none of those compared to what she had seen when her head turned involuntarily toward the fighting that afternoon. She'd seen Haydn's arm extended, the man in front of him dropping his own weapon before he fell. Later, she watched as her husband wiped his sword clean. That blood, she'd thought, was of the man now lying dead on the road. Or wherever they were now. Isaac had taken her ahead while Holt and Haydn stayed behind for some time. Had they put their bodies in the nearby woods? Buried them? How could they do such a thing without shovels?

"You are still in shock," he said. Phillipa did not deny it. "We will sleep separately," he said, his voice flat.

When she looked into his eyes, blue-grey and clear, Phillipa had no notion of whether his proclamation was because of the attack, or the question he'd asked her this morning.

She'd never answered. What could she have said? Would she admit that, were she to ignore her father's directive, her sister would pay the price?

So instead, she had said nothing.

"'Tis probably for the best." Phillipa took another bite of the tart.

"Agreed," her husband said, turning back to his brother.

THE REMAINDER of the meal passed in a kind of quiet contentment Phillipa had never known before. At home, as at court, she'd always been expected to be someone other. Here, no one asked for anything from her, except pleasant conversation.

She'd learned the Lord and Lady of Brookhurst had four children, close in age to Phillipa, though all were away at present. Most interesting, however, was the story the lady had shared about their marriage. Apparently Lady Kristine was once a lady's maid and had met her husband when he and Haydn's uncle visited her overlord's castle.

"A love match," she said, in awe. Phillipa had heard of so few of them at court, at least among nobles. She had never considered marrying for love before, not seriously. Of course she'd heard tales of such—stories and songs that told of a love that most would never enjoy. Among the queen's ladies, only one was fanciful enough to believe such a thing truly possible.

"You seem more surprised by that than our difference in stations," Lady Kristine said.

"I suppose both surprise me," she admitted, their tones low enough not to be overheard by the men to their right and left. Haydn was occupied with his brother, and Lord Brookhurst spoke now to a servant.

"You shall be even more surprised to meet your new husband's family. 'Tis often said they must be either blessed, or cursed."

Phillipa didn't understand. "Blessed, or cursed?"

"Aye, for the love matches in their family. You've heard of his parents meeting, have you not?"

"Aye." She knew little except that Haydn's father had been a reiver, but she did not want to admit as much. What should she say? That he did not trust her, with good reason, and so hardly spoke to her except when 'twas necessary?

"And of his uncle Bryce?"

Again she knew only a bit of their story. "Aye, he's made mention of him."

"For every Waryn, there is a love match."

"Every one?" It was not possible.

"Aye. My husband first met your new sister-in-law, Lady Emma, when he lived with her husband for a time. He was betrothed to another, in fact."

"Then how were they able to wed?"

Lady Kristine leaned forward. "The bride-to-be was in love with another man, and enceinte with his child."

Phillipa gasped, her hand covering her mouth. "Nay?"

"Lady Kristine," Haydn interrupted; Phillipa had not

realized he could hear them, "could tell tales of my family's exploits all eve. If not for the events of a long day, we would welcome them."

"Of course," Lady Kristine said. "You must be weary from travel." She knew not of the attack. "And just your third night as husband and wife, I am told. As such, I took the liberty of placing your bedchambers beside each other. A hot bath is awaiting you." She leaned forward to address Holt. "And for you as well, Holt."

Phillipa watched her husband to see if he would correct her, but since they still had separate chambers, it seemed that was well enough for him. He thanked Lady Kristine and waited for her to give permission for them to rise as the hosts apparently intended to stay at the meal. When she did, Phillipa stood, her chair pulled out by a servant from behind.

"Enjoy a bath and soft bed. I know all too well the toils of travelling a distance such as on your journey to Rymerden Castle."

Rymerden Castle? "We travel to—"

"Many thanks," her husband interrupted her. "We bid you a good eve."

Holt, it seemed, was staying a bit longer.

"I should speak to you," Haydn said to Lord Brookhurst, "after I partake in your wife's generous offer of a hot bath."

"Ask my steward where to find me," Brookhurst said. "Good eve to you both."

With that, and with a final glance to their hosts, and to Holt, she accepted the offer of her husband's arm. It was only after they'd passed under the archway of the hall's main entrance that Haydn let her go as if she were a leper.

They followed the waiting maid, not saying a word to each other. Phillipa wished their accommodations were in separate towers rather than just next to each other. That's when she realized what Haydn had been doing from the start. Putting distance between them, knowing 'twas easier that way. Certainly the more she learned of him, the more she watched him and, sometimes, even caught him looking at her, the more she began to wish theirs was a love match too. Or at least a marriage not plagued by mistrust and competing concerns.

A marriage doomed to fail.

# CHAPTER

# FOURTEEN

"It sounds to me as if you've not truly spoken to her."

Haydn extended his legs in front of him. Ale in hand, the warmth of Conrad's fire in his solar chamber, now devoid of any light but that which was provided by candles and two wall torches, it was the first time since he'd arrived at court he felt relaxed.

Certainly he wouldn't use that word to describe his time at court. Or his interactions with Phillipa. Whenever they were together he alternated between fear she'd learn something to use against his family, desire for a woman who'd each day begun to shed the weight of impossible expectations she'd clearly lived under with her father, and annoyance with himself for caring.

"We've spoken plenty," he said. After explaining the situation to his uncle's friend, a man who could be trusted with the dilemma, Haydn had waited for him to agree on the course of action he was taking. Instead, Conrad hesitated.

Mimicking his position, his host sat back in his own velvet-cushioned chair. "The last time I was with your father, he told me something he'd likely not care for me to repeat to you. But I've never been known for discretion."

"Nay, you have not," he agreed dryly. Haydn braced for his next words.

"'He is the strongest of all my sons,'" Conrad said. "'Here,'" he pointed to his sword arm, "'but not here.'" He pointed to his heart. "'He will never be hurt by a woman because none will get close enough to him for such a thing.'"

Hardly a revelation. His father and mother both, and Haddie even, had said the same many times. But this was very different. "She did not deny being a spy for her father. Indeed, it is the very reason we were forced to wed."

"Do you have reason to believe her loyalty to the king will be stronger than to you?"

"She hardly knows me."

"Of your doing, it seems."

"Knowing her is too dangerous a proposition."

"It would seem not knowing her is more so."

Holt had made a similar argument. But what should he do? Trust a woman who could not deny she would turn on him the very first chance she had? "You know Edward as well as I. If he thinks Phillipa disloyal to him, or that she does not do her duty to the crown, it is possible he will punish her sister. I don't think she gives a damn about that bastard father of hers. At least, she shouldn't. But she would do anything for the young woman, not yet married, who could be easily ruined. And it is my guess that is the leverage they have over Phillipa."

"There is more than one way to climb a mountain. If 'tis too steep, go around it. If the path around too long, find another route."

Haydn took a deep swig of ale. "Or avoid the mountain completely."

Conrad laughed. "Good luck, my son. If you can avoid that lovely wife of yours, you are a better man than I."

It hadn't been easy. "I should retire," he said. "We leave at dawn."

Conrad stood, and Haydn did the same.

"I will see you off in the morn," he said.

Nodding in parting, Haydn had nearly reached the door before Conrad said, "Go to her."

He glanced back over his shoulder and caught the man's eye, knowing this afternoon's attack was an excuse not to do so. If anything, he should take Conrad's advice for that reason. His wife had been clearly shaken. "Good eve, Conrad."

By the time he reached his chamber, Haydn still hadn't come to a decision. He'd not planned to remain celibate on this journey. Certainly he'd not expected to desire his own wife. But the fact complicated matters. He'd told her too much already.

*You don't need to reveal your life story, Haydn. But you can not beget an heir if you avoid her all the way to Hillside.*

He pulled off his boots, preparing to bed down. Haydn would think more on the matter tomorrow. For now, he should sleep. Unfortunately, as he lay on the bed watching the candlelight flicker beside his bed, his eyes would not shut.

He thought back to the attack. It did not matter that they attacked first. Killing a man should never, as his father once said, be taken lightly. Not even in battle. He and Holt had buried the bodies, had even said a few words over their shallow graves as their father would have expected them to do.

Graves they needed to dig because he, and Holt, had ended their time in this world.

What must Phillipa be thinking now? Unlike him, she'd never be forced to face such a gruesome scene. Haydn swung his legs off the bed, grabbed the single candle by its brass holder, and made his way to the door. Listening, he heard nothing. She was very likely asleep, as she'd been the night before.

He would open the door. If she was sleeping, he'd leave.

And if she was not?

Opening it, he walked through the threshold, almost willing her to be slumbering, not trusting himself otherwise. Surely he hadn't been expecting the sight that greeted him. His wife sat in front of the hearth, a fire similar to his giving off the only light in the chamber. Goblet in hand, dressed in a shift, Phillipa did not hear him open the door. She must be deep in thought. Did she think of him?

"Phillipa?"

She startled.

"I am not here for any other reason than to ensure you are well."

That did seem to put his wife at ease. What horrors had she been told about "relations," as she called them, between men and women? Had she ever kissed a man before?

He immediately tossed aside the thought.

"Lady Kristine had this sent to me." She raised her goblet. "'Tis as fine a wine as I've ever tasted. I was told, after we had been betrothed, I'd not ever drink wine again. That in the North they drink only ale. Is that true?"

Spying the flagon on top of a wooden cupboard made for just the purpose, he made his way toward it. An array of goblets and even remnants of bread and cheese remained.

Many noblemen, and women, entertained in the bedchamber, though he preferred to reserve it for other activities. "We drink the blood of the animals we hunt," he said, sitting in the seat next to her. Both were large, ornate wooden chairs, comfortably lined with bright crimson velvet cushions.

"I had heard that of the Scots."

He took a sip of wine. "And I'm told many things about court, most of which are likely untrue. For instance, does the groom of the stool know more of the king's mind than even his wife?"

Phillipa laughed. "There are many who know the king's mind more than his wife. The groom of the stool included," she added.

"I knew it to be true. Do you know the man?"

"Aye, I do."

"I don't envy his position."

"I don't envy most servants' positions."

He was thoughtful for a moment. "Some are treated better than others."

"But none have the freedom afforded to those who happened to be born into nobility, as you and I have."

"My sister would say women, even those born into nobility, have little freedom that isn't given to them by men." His sister oft complained of the limitations of her gender. Once she marched up to the altar just after mass and, as brazen as could be, touched it, despite women being forbidden to do such a thing. It had caused a scandal, but then, Haddie was not known to care about doing so.

"I would agree with her. How old is your sister?"

"Ten and nine. The youngest of us all."

"A similar age to my own."

So quickly the conversation turned. Any discussion of

Lady Catherine would be laced with an undertone he wasn't willing to endure at this moment. So Haydn changed topics, thinking of Conrad's advice. "You seemed to enjoy the apricot tart at supper."

"Very much. Sweets have always brought me enjoyment."

"What else brings you enjoyment, Phillipa?" He had not meant the question to sound so flirtatious, but it had come out that way nonetheless.

"Riding Lady. Being with my sister. When I attended the queen, I enjoyed dancing very much."

"Do you not dance in your own hall?"

"Nay. My father does not like the distraction. He enjoys his musicians well enough, but dancing? Nay."

"My mother enjoys it as well. If there is an occasion to dance, she will find it. Kenshire's hall is known for more celebrations than anywhere in Northumbria."

"Do you enjoy it?"

Haydn would not qualify it as enjoyable, but neither did he despise it, as her father seemed to. She looked so hopeful for his answer, it didn't seem to matter that they'd have little occasion to dance together as they would reside many miles apart. But this moment, they were in the same chamber. So he stood and, despite his good judgment, reached out his hand.

"But. . . there are no musicians."

"Neither are they required to dance."

She hesitated. And then stood, taking his hand. The moment she did, Haydn knew for certain he'd just made a terrible decision. But it was too late now. Instead, he encircled her waist with his free hand, and still holding the other, he began to move.

"You dance so well."

"You seem surprised." He avoided looking at her, instead spinning Phillipa again.

"When I asked if you enjoyed it, you seemed hesitant."

As Phillipa and Haydn moved, the crackle of the fire was their song. "My mother ensured we were all proficient at it, whether we enjoyed it or nay."

"I could not imagine such a thing."

He spun them as wide as he was able, navigating the chairs on which they'd just been sitting. "Being forced to dance?"

"Having a mother."

She said it as if they still spoke about the wine or something similarly mundane. As if it were nothing more than a fact rather than a devastating truth. Haydn slowed, despite himself. "Phillipa. . ."

"That is to say, having her still. When she was alive, our lives were different. She was a buffer, of sorts, between. . ." She stopped, maybe noticing they'd stopped too.

"Between you and your father?"

Phillipa nodded. "I miss her so much sometimes 'tis difficult to breathe if I think long enough or allow the memories to flood my mind."

He'd thought her eyes were brown. But this close, he could see that was only partially true. His wife's brown eyes were clear, guileless.

"Have you ever been kissed before, Phillipa?"

Haydn guessed her heart raced as quickly as his own. "Aye."

"Good." He lowered his head, cursing himself the whole time. Consummating their vows and wooing his wife were two very different things. He needed to do the former, not the latter. Despite it, Haydn watched as she raised her chin and closed her eyes as if preparing to taste something sour.

He'd have laughed if his body hadn't already begun preparing for what was to come. If he had not spent the past three nights lying awake for too long, imagining how her lips would feel. How they would taste.

He was about to find out.

# CHAPTER
# FIFTEEN

H is wife's eyes were closed, her shoulders, tense. This was not the way. "I've been in battle with men less fearful of the onslaught they were about to endure." He said to her as Phillipa's eyes flew open. "You said you've been kissed before?"

"I have."

"Tell me."

"You must be jesting."

"I assure you, Phillipa. I am not." His hand dropped to the side, and they were no longer in dancing position. In fact, there was more space between them now than ever.

"I. . ." She hesitated. "I have been kissed at court. More than once."

Haydn tried hard not to smile. "Did you enjoy it?"

She shrugged. "Once I hardly felt it at all."

"Then that was not a kiss."

"His lips touched mine."

"Irrelevant."

"Another time, I was taken unaware, preparing for a

private discussion, and instead found myself fending off an overly amorous suitor."

Now there were two men he might have to kill.

"The third was horrible. He attempted to put his tongue in my mouth."

"Did he, now?"

"Indeed. When I asked the other ladies about it, they assured me 'twas normal. But I had not really wanted to repeat the experience."

"That is all? Three kisses?"

"Mmm, no. Four. Just this summer a stablehand who had professed his love for me when I returned from Westminster suddenly kissed me after handing me Lady's reins."

"He forced himself on you?"

"Not precisely. I believe he'd been as surprised as I at his forwardness and immediately pulled away, apologetic." Haydn crossed the stablehand off his list. "Why do you wish to know about my kisses?"

"To understand better why you are so scared. So let me tell you, wife, what to expect from me. I do intend to use my tongue"—she made a face—"to entice you to consummate our marriage this eve."

Phillipa—his sweet, quiet, demure Phillipa—placed her hands on her hips. "There is naught," she declared, "you could do with your *tongue* that would make me wish to consummate our marriage."

Oh, how wrong she was.

"If you do not ask for it, we shall not do so this eve. Do we have a deal?"

Her hands remained in place. "Unless I ask for. . ."

"Relations."

She did smile then. "Relations. I will remain a virgin this eve?"

"Aye. You will."

She nodded, so satisfied with her pact, so unaware, that Haydn could not have been more pleased with their "deal."

He closed the gap between them. Her hands dropped.

He cupped her face. Her eyes widened.

He lowered his head. Phillipa did not stand a chance.

At the first touch of their lips, she startled. Haydn resisted groaning at the simple touch so as not to scare her away. When he felt her shoulders relax, he began to take up the challenge. Running his tongue along the folds of her lips, as soon as she opened for him, Haydn took charge.

Moving his hands from her cheeks down to her shoulders, he coaxed her own tongue to his. When she touched him, so very tentative, he dropped his hands again, this time to her waist. Meanwhile, he showed her the dance. At first she simply touched her tongue to him, and then retreated it.

But he was a patient man.

Again his hands slipped, this time to cup her backside, pulling her toward him. If the press of them together scared her, Phillipa gave no indication of it. Finally she trusted him enough to give herself over completely.

That's when he widened his mouth, delving deeper and deeper. Instead of a simple touch, now his hands moved of their own accord. Molding and pressing, Haydn somehow continued to hold back a groan. That might alert her to how affected he was, if the press of their groins together did not do so already. An innocent, she did not yet understand.

But she would.

By now Phillipa was no longer solely a bystander. She gripped his shoulders as if to hold on. Opened her mouth more widely, tangled with his tongue more readily. Their kiss could not be deepened, so instead he simply continued, over and over and over, to draw her in, and out. Just as he would when they finally joined together.

When she asked.

"Haydn?" His wife pulled back long enough to look at him. The question was one of the first from her he could easily answer.

"That is a kiss, my lady. And the longing you feel. . ." He allowed one hand to slip over her hips, along her thigh. "One tug and this shift could be easily removed."

"And then?"

"And then I will explore you first with my hands. Then with my mouth."

Still breathing heavily from their kiss, she swallowed.

"And then?"

"You will be a virgin no longer, Phillipa."

Returning to his own bedchamber now would be more difficult than saddling his horse to journey to London to take this woman as his wife. He could not trust her. Had not asked for her.

But in this moment, he'd never wanted anything more than to consummate his marriage to Lady Phillipa of Sherfield. When she nodded, Haydn didn't hesitate for a second. Gripping the hem of her shift with both hands, he pulled it off with the deftness of a lady's maid. Unsurprisingly, she wore nothing under it. Rarely did one wear anything to sleep.

On full display before him, Phillipa attempted to cover her breasts with her hands. Instead, he encircled both wrists, held them by her side, and lowered his mouth to her breast. He let go of one wrist long enough to cup her breast just as his mouth covered her and Phillipa gasped. Haydn's goal. . . to make her forget she was nervous.

To that end, he circled her nipple with his tongue,

closing his eyes as his wife's hands entangled themselves in his hair. After giving both breasts the same attention, he reached between her legs, not allowing her time to be embarrassed. She did jolt away from his touch, not surprisingly.

What did surprise him was how wet his wife was already. And how quickly Phillipa apparently overcame her shyness as her hand covered his, encouraging him. As his finger moved, slowly at first, his mouth moved upward, to her neck, and finally, claimed her lips once more.

His tongue and fingers in perfect sync.

He almost felt bad for the onslaught, knowing she'd not last long. And she didn't. Now gripping his shoulders once again, she squeezed and moaned against his lips. But Haydn didn't stop there. He knew how to give a woman pleasure, and he'd use those skills now to ensure Phillipa never again wondered if the marital act was something to dread or desire.

*You will hardly see her after this journey.*

Shoving away the thought, he cupped her with his palm, and it was enough. Clenching around his fingers, Phillipa broke their kiss to breathe. To relish in her very first release, one he was oddly pleased to have given her. He pulled away, watching his wife.

He disrobed as she stared at him, confused and curious. As she began to breathe normally again, Haydn slipped off his boots.

She was perfect.

"There are many ways," Haydn said, his voice surprisingly unsteady, "for you to find release." Tossing his tunic onto the floor, he paused. And then dropped the woolen hose as well.

"Haydn." She stared at him as he sprang free. "What do you think to do with that?"

# CHAPTER
# SIXTEEN

She'd never seen a male nude before.

Despite the brief kisses at court, Phillipa had never had the occasion to be alone with one for any length of time. First, the revelation that she'd not truly ever been kissed. And then, what her husband had just done to her. And now this?

"'Tis not the reaction most men would hope for, Phillipa."

His tone was light. Teasing. But she was not. "I know enough to understand that is supposed to go inside me, but certainly such a thing is not possible." Nor did she wish it to be.

"Did you enjoy what we just shared?"

Her eyes flew from Haydn's groin to his mouth. The one that had covered hers just moments ago. Still she could not reconcile the feeling he wrought in her, so different than those other kisses, if, indeed, they could be called such.

Phillipa wanted him to kiss her again. She wanted him to touch her again. She wanted him to continue to stare at her body as if she were the goddess Venus, as he'd done since the moment her shift was removed.

"Aye. Very much," she admitted, not feeling particularly coy.

"Do you trust me?"

Her eyes sought his. Phillipa didn't answer.

"Do you trust me not to hurt you?" he amended.

She did, and was sorry she could not answer his first question. This was no way to begin a marriage. And yet, what choice did she have? But aye, she trusted him not to hurt her.

"I do."

In response, he took her hand. The gentle touch from such a man, the same one who'd slayed their attackers, who had muscles in places she couldn't imagine even existed. . . Phillipa swallowed. He led her to the bed, and when she pulled the coverlet down and stepped onto the stool, watching as he closed the curtains so they were completely closed off from any chill, she was no longer scared.

In fact, when her head hit the pillow as she lay down, Phillipa grew curious. Surely it would not feel the way his fingers had. She'd been shocked at the touch, as shocked as what her husband did with his tongue. That kiss could have lasted a lifetime and she'd offer no complaint.

When he lay next to her on his side, Haydn's hand propping up his head, she wasn't sure what to expect, but surely it was not his fingers winding through strands of her hair.

"I saw your hair first," he said. "As you walked toward us, and I could finally see your face, I was struck by how serene you looked. As if you'd accepted what was to come."

"Because I had. My marriage was never to be my own."

"Hmmm." Haydn reached out, his fingertips just barely touching her shoulder.

"You were angry," she said, remembering his expression. "'Twas what I noticed first."

"Holt chastised me for not hiding my thoughts from the king more clearly. But then, he knew this would upset me, and my family. There was no use pretending otherwise."

When his fingers trailed a path down her arm, then slipping coyly over to her breast, she held her breath. He encircled her nipple, and she could not help but watch the effect. It was now hard from his touch. "You've done this many times before." It was not an accusation, just a fact.

"I have."

Her eyes flew to his. There was a tempest there, so different from his gentle touch. She could not discern what he could possibly be thinking. "Are you this way with me, because of my father? Or with everyone?"

His fingers began to explore again.

"Which way?"

"Indiscernible."

"Everyone," he said. "But you especially."

For some reason his open admission made her smile. Now her husband's hand was splayed on her stomach. She groaned, thinking what he might do next. Sure enough, his hand did not remain in place for long.

"I wish it were not so," she admitted.

"As do I.'

"Do you truly?"

He grabbed her inner thigh and pulled it toward him, spreading her legs wider.

"Of course." When his hand reached her core, Haydn stopped. Rested it there on that very intimate part of her. "I'd have a marriage like my parents, if given the choice."

"A love match."

"Aye."

"You do not strike me as the kind of man who pines for love."

She thrust her hips into his hand, encouraging him. But still, it remained in place.

"Every person alive pines for love, Phillipa. What else is there? Land? Power? Without love, such things are meaningless."

Her brows drew together. "You would not do well at court."

"No," he agreed, ignoring her prompting. "I would not."

It struck her that, if there were a man most unlike her father in this world, it was her husband.

"When you smile, I can almost believe we are husband and wife in truth. I like your smile, Phillipa."

What precisely did that mean? That they would not consummate their marriage yet? Was that not why they lay in this bed? Again, she jerked her hips upward, but he ignored her. So Phillipa took her hand, placed it on his arm, and moved it downward, prompting him.

"When you wish to say something, do so."

That again. "I can not."

"Aye, you can."

Phillipa didn't have the words. She shook her head. In response, Haydn's hand stilled.

Ahhh. She could not take such torture any longer. "Touch me. Like you did before."

He did. Haydn was less gentle this time too. His fingers plunged into her, his palm cupping her still. Phillipa closed her eyes, knowing this time what was to come. As before, she moved with the rhythm of his hand. Faster and faster still. And then. . . he was gone.

Her eyes flew open. And in that brief span, her husband had moved lightning fast. No longer beside her, he was above her now. Guiding himself into her. She was too surprised to know what to say. What to do. Surely it would not fit. Surely, this would hurt.

"You know when I break your barrier, there will be pain?"

She nodded. "Aye." The sensation of him inside her was a very different one than his fingers. She thought, perhaps, it would be the same.

"But then there will be no pain. I promise, Phillipa."

She braced herself for it. And just like that, she was no longer a virgin. He'd thrusted, past her barrier, and then stilled, buried inside her. Phillipa's eyes were squeezed shut. Her fingers dug into his arms. Or attempted to, at least. It was like gripping the steel of a sword, if less sharp than still smooth and hard.

"Does it still hurt?"

Opening her eyes, she nearly gasped. Gone was the mistrust. The anger. The reticence. Her husband's expression was of genuine concern. Caring even.

"Nay, it does not."

His features relaxed. Became more guarded once again. And then, he began to move. Slowly, at first.

His hand reached between them.

"Why do you do that?" she said as he pressed and circled her with his fingers. The dual sensation made her forget the question. Not care about the answer. Soon she was moving with him to a rhythm she never knew existed.

Phillipa allowed her hands to explore then. She ran them over his shoulders, felt the muscles there as they flexed with each and every thrust. When he pulled his hand away and leaned down to kiss her, Phillipa welcomed the touch. Wanted to feel his lips again. Reveled in the touch of his tongue to hers.

This time when she began to tense, when her buttocks clenched, she knew what was coming. Allowing it, allowing *him,* opened a door she could not close. As spasms wracked her, his kiss deepening, Phillipa pulled her husband close. The touch of his chest to hers only helped to intensify wave after wave.

Haydn tore his mouth from hers, tossed his head back and made the kind of sound that made Phillipa wish they were just starting rather than ending. She had never, in her life, witnessed such virility before. He pumped into her one last time, his eyes settling on her.

Phillipa could not look away. She had no real notion of what, truly, had just happened between them. But she did know one thing for certain.

"I wish to do that again."

# CHAPTER
# SEVENTEEN

I t had been two days since that night.

Two long, miserable, rainy days. Haydn was unsure if he looked forward more to being dry or having another opportunity to make love to his wife.

He waited for her as she and Holt rode up to the fortified manor, no longer unsure. Despite the incessant rain and muddy roads, along with their overly slow progress, his pulse quickened as she approached. Even knowing how dangerous his thoughts were, he refused to shove them aside but renewed his vow not to reveal anything to her that could be used against his family.

*Which means not getting so close.*

But since that night, something had shifted. Something they'd not had the opportunity to explore. Their pace had put last evening's planned accommodations out of reach, so with no other choice, they'd stayed outside in the elements with trees as their cover. With their wool cloaks no longer effective against the rain, they'd spent a long night in the best shelter he'd been able to provide. He'd at least been able to form a makeshift bed under a rock overhang large enough for Phillipa. She stayed dry, of sorts, until this morn. When the rain had finally stopped earlier, none were rejoicing. Not until the manor came into view.

"What is this place?" Isaac asked, riding up to him.

Haydn looked up to the gatehouse, removing his mantle so they might see the tunic he wore beneath it, one which bore the Kenshire crest. He'd planned to reach Caldmoor Priory, which had accommodated him on their journey to London. But again, the weather, as it was wont to do, wreaked havoc on their plans.

"According to the travelers we met earlier, it is the home of a DeBurg. The baron apparently had been a squire for King Henry, who knighted him on Christmas day and made the man his private counsellor."

"An interesting tale. With luck, he will welcome us."

"I would see no reason he would not."

It was considered an affront not to welcome travelers, even ones who might typically be adversaries. Though there was no reason to think of the man as such, Haydn did find it odd that such a manor house would be so far from any village or town, but it suited their purposes. The sun would set on their drenched party, and he did not wish Phillipa to be chilled.

What she and his brother spoke of, he did not know. Hamon rode behind them.

Turning toward the two-story gatehouse, Haydn waited for the gate to rise. Built on slightly raised ground on the river's basin, its crenellated curtain wall was shaped in a near-perfect circle.

The gate rose just as Phillipa reached him. As she'd done these past two days, his wife looked at him as if. . . as if they'd consummated their marriage. And more. Twice more that night after she gave her virginity to him they were together. Before the sun rose, he'd lifted her head from his chest and dressed, standing over her for so long he was sure she would wake.

As he'd done then, Haydn thought of what to say. How to proceed. He'd lain with enough women to know theirs was no simple coupling. Every time she'd looked at him, that eve and since, it was as if Phillipa wanted to tell him something.

And he was fairly certain what that something was. When she paused that night after he asked if she trusted him, Haydn knew. She had no cause to do so, because he'd been deceiving her from the start. Was deceiving her now. And perhaps he had no other choice, but maybe, he did.

Anything she'd been about to say was cut off by a stablehand who met them in the courtyard. There were less than twenty earls in England, his father and Phillipa's two of them. So he was not surprised the crest had been recognized, gaining them entry. But Haydn was grateful for it.

"I will take your mounts, my lord. My lady."

"Many thanks," he said dismounting. Before he could assist Phillipa, she was on the ground as well. The woman did navigate her way around Lady as well as any he knew, even his aunt Catrina.

The courtyard was small, and mostly empty as light rain had begun to fall again. Hurrying toward the keep, Haydn was grateful when the wooden door was opened as they ascended the stone stairs. A bald man, similar in age to his father, stood in the center. "Welcome to Caldwell Manor, my lord," he said, bowing ever so slightly. "I am John, the steward here, and glad to offer lodging for the eve."

"I am Lord Waryn, first baron Waryn and son of the Earl of Kenshire. This is my wife, Lady Phillipa, daughter of Earl

Sherfield, and my brother, Sir Holt of Kenshire. These are our men, Sir Isaac and Sir Hamon."

The steward bowed again to his wife. "My lady. Do come inside." A modest hall, also mostly empty, sat before them. "God took the lord of Caldwell this past winter. As you can see, we do not often entertain travellers."

"Is the lady of the manor in residence?" Phillipa asked him.

"Nay, she passed more than ten years ago. Lord and Lady Caldwell left no issue behind. We await the king's orders."

That explained much. "We are sorry for your loss, Master John."

After exchanging greetings with his men, their entire party was brought to the second floor. "We've many rooms unoccupied. Shall I show you each to one, or. . ." He looked between Phillipa and Haydn.

All eyes were on him. Haydn didn't hesitate. "I sleep with my wife."

While the steward bid Phillipa and the men to follow him, Holt pulled Haydn behind. "I knew something was different after Brookhurst. And then the last two days. You've been speaking to her more. The looks between you." Holt slapped his forehead. "You are well and truly married."

He did not confirm or deny it. "It was you who told me I was too harsh with her."

"I never liked your plan but care for it even less now."

Haydn wanted to tell Holt something had passed between them. That he felt more protective of her than ever. And each day, as she asked less and less for permission to share what was on her mind, her eyes no longer going to his when she was asked a question, he could sense their closeness growing.

But his brother was too young to offer the advice Haydn needed. He may look like a man, and swing a sword like a man, but just three years earlier his brother had still been fostering with their Uncle Neill.

"Her father advises the same king who threatened to strip our parents of Kenshire," he reminded him, a refrain that had run through his mind over and over again. When he caught himself watching her. Admiring her. Wanting her.

"You did not marry her father."

"Pardon me, Lord Waryn." The steward had returned. "Lady Phillipa is there," he pointed toward the end of the hall, "I will have a meal sent to you after your bath."

He'd never wanted a hot bath more. "Thank you, Master John."

The man nodded. "Your wife said there was no need for a chambermaid despite that none seem to be traveling with you."

His fault. But the thought that Phillipa wanted privacy wasn't one he'd disagree with. "I will attend to her. Again, our sincerest thank you for your hospitality. If there is anything I can do for you in return, please do let me know."

The steward hesitated. "I do not wish to burden my lord..."

"You've been most gracious hosting us without notice. Please, you are no burden."

Holt looked at him as if to say Mother would be proud of his manners. Which, of course, she would. Nothing pleased her more than when one of her children displayed the grace she said was a hallmark of the Caiser name. Haydn would have loved to meet his grandfather. He'd heard so many tales of the man.

"If you would speak to me briefly in the morn, I do have a boon to ask of you. After you break your fast, perhaps?"

"Of course," Haydn assured him. "If you will excuse me—"

"Pardon, my lord, for keeping you. Come, Sir Holt. You will wish to dry off and take a meal. I have just the servant to assist you."

His brother's coy smile had Haydn shaking his head. If Mother would be pleased by their manners, she'd not take kindly to the activities his brother would no doubt be engaged in this eve. If he did not foster a child out of wedlock before he wed, their mother often said, she would thank the Blessed Mary for it.

"Enjoy your evening," Holt said much too cheerily. But as he sauntered away with their gracious host, Haydn found himself scurrying to the end of the hall. To his wife. He needed to ask her some difficult questions, ones he likely did not want the answer to. But when he opened the door and spied her already in the tub Master John must have had prepared when he saw them coming, Haydn changed his mind about the discussion he needed to have with Phillipa.

First—he closed the door with a thud—he needed a bath.

# CHAPTER
# EIGHTEEN

"Surely you do not mean to join me?"

It seemed, however, her husband intended just that. Her father had never let her or her sister join a hunt. Plenty of other women did so, but not them. So she'd never had the occasion to know what it was like to stalk an animal. But she could very much guess it may have looked like Haydn coming toward her now. With each step, another piece of his clothing fell to the floor.

"It is a large enough tub for four people," he said, continuing to disrobe.

"I was surprised by its size. It must have taken many servants to fill." Phillipa lowered herself deeper into the water, still shy despite their wedding night. "Did you know the king had taps of hot and cold water installed at Westminster for his baths?"

Her husband chose that moment to remove the last of his clothing. With the fire and candles placed all throughout the large bedchamber, she could see him easily. This time, more prepared than before, Phillipa could also appreciate that every man surely did not look like him.

"You must spend many hours in the training yard," she blurted, watching as the muscles in his shoulders and arms bulged as he used them to prop himself into the tub. "You are so very. . . naked," she added, getting one last look before he submerged himself.

Sitting across from her, Haydn extended his legs so they straddled hers. Phillipa repositioned her feet and then, when one touched him in the groin accidently, she attempted to quickly move it away. But he was too quick. Capturing it as he grabbed the herb-scented sponge left on the side of the tub, her husband began to wash her.

Phillipa had been assisted in the tub many times by servants, but this was something different entirely. His movements were slow and sensual. Deliberate, as his fingers "slipped" from the sponge to brush against her skin.

"You dismissed the maid," he asked. "Why?"

Without her own lady's maid, Phillipa should have kept the woman for the duration of her bath. But she hadn't and her husband knew why.

"I. . ."

"Say it, Phillipa."

"Would you have me say every thought that pops into my head?"

He didn't hesitate. "Aye, I would."

If she did that, Haydn would not be pleased. She put those more serious thoughts to the side for now. "I bid her leave knowing you would join me in our chamber."

"You wanted privacy."

"Aye."

"Why?"

Oh, he was deplorable. "Why do you do that?"

He moved the sponge slowly up her inner thigh. "This?"

She clenched in anticipation. "Nay. Why do you force me to say things?"

Haydn's hands froze. "I do not, nor will I, force you to do anything, Phillipa. You've your own mind, and will."

"Cajole then," she amended.

He resumed his illicit ministrations "Because, with every word you utter, without consequence, you learn I welcome your thoughts."

"Even if they are ones you do not agree with?"

Haydn leaned forward in the tub. "Aye. Even those."

Haydn would surely not welcome some of her thoughts. But when an incredibly seductive husband bathed you, as the water lapped each time he moved and the fire crackled its approval, 'twas not the time to share *those* thoughts.

"And yet, you so rarely share your own."

Aye, she was the prey indeed. The look on Haydn's face would scare virgin Phillipa. But no longer. Indeed, she welcomed it, knowing now what she did not two days before. Water splashed onto the floor as Haydn re-positioned himself, his body now covering hers, his manhood brushing her stomach, and Phillipa gripped the sides of the tub.

"Since you successfully evaded my question, let me tell you what I think, Phillipa." Her name itself was a flirtation of its own. "I think you dismissed the maid because you wanted us to be alone. So that I might do this." His hand reached between them. "Mmm." He slipped one finger, and then two, inside. "So ready for me." Her eyes closed as he touched her, but then his fingers were gone much too soon. "As I am for you."

Taking her right hand and guiding it from the side of the tub, dipping it beneath the water, Haydn placed it on him, showing her what to do. He guided her up and down his length. More water escaped from the tub, and Phillipa reached down with her second hand.

Somehow, this felt more intimate than being in bed. Haydn's eyes never left hers, and though she wanted him to kiss her, she very much enjoyed seeing his expression too as she mimicked the movements he'd shown her.

She was doing this to him. "This is why women are forbidden such acts."

Haydn's mouth opened but he said nothing. Phillipa was certain he didn't understand her meaning. But she understood now the church's stance. What power she held at this very moment.

Phillipa reached up, deciding not to wait for him, and kissed him. For a brief moment she panicked, thinking he might not respond. Or kiss her back, in turn. But her fears were for naught. Her hands forgot to keep moving as Haydn's mouth covered hers, their tongues finding each other instantly.

She was so lost in the kiss that Phillipa only realized her hands had fallen from him and were now back to the side of the tub as Haydn guided himself into her. Welcoming him, indeed, thrusting her hips to meet his length, they created wave after wave, moving together in perfect rhythm.

She was surprised when he pulled his head back to look at her. Even more surprising, Phillipa was not embarrassed. Instead, she met his gaze. As his hips circled, and then slowed, she forgot to breathe.

"You are so very beautiful, Phillipa."

Not expecting those words, she had no response. Phillipa could have just as easily complimented her husband in return. But the words did not come. Instead, she replayed his words in her mind as he increased the pace between them.

He thought her beautiful.

What a trivial thing to care about given what was between them. Given the treacherous purpose for their union. But she couldn't pretend his words didn't affect her. They did, signifying a vulnerability in Haydn she hadn't been sure he possessed.

When he lowered his head again, the thought that he'd stopped kissing her to say those words to her. . . she began to spasm, every bit of her body shuddering with release. Haydn pulled away once more, cried out her name and pumped into her one last time.

They stayed that way for a long while, neither saying a word. Or even moving. Until her husband finally looked into her eyes once more.

"Phillipa, we need to talk."

# CHAPTER
## NINETEEN

If he was a lesser man, Haydn might have become offended last eve when his wife, for the second time in as many days, fell asleep prematurely. After their bath, after he'd dried her off quite thoroughly, something he'd never done to a woman before. Haydn decided he never wished to bathe alone again.

Which was, of course, at the very root of the problem with their marriage. Any fool could tell him, even if he were loath to admit it to himself, the past few days had altered their plans. What he couldn't determine just yet, however, was how to proceed.

Finding his brother's chamber, Haydn knocked. When Holt finally came to the door, he wasn't surprised to find his brother disheveled.

"It's not dawn already?"

"Do you see light streaming from the embrasures in your bedchamber?" Holt stepped aside as Haydn entered the room. Unsurprisingly, there was no maid there. Holt rarely slept with the women he bedded. "So your bedmate is gone?"

His brother moved to the basin by his bed. "How can you be sure she was here for an extended time?" Holt splashed his face.

Haydn declined to answer.

"Why precisely are you about before daybreak? So anxious to get back on the muddy road?"

In fact, he was not. "Nay, but we must leave at dawn. We will make our way back onto the Old North Road."

Holt looked at him oddly. "Father dislikes it for the excessive amount of travellers. And the possibility of trouble that comes along with it."

Avoiding major roads when they travelled was something their father had always advised, but with it came less places to stay that were not out of doors. "I would not have Phillipa sleep among the elements again." When his brother gaped at him, Haydn added, "Besides, I can not imagine more trouble than we've already encountered *not* taking the old Roman road."

"That was unfortunate," Holt agreed. "But unusual enough an occurrence. I do not believe it will happen again."

"Not so unusual that we've never been attacked before."

"Unprovoked?"

Holt dried his face. "Tensions run high since Lochmaben."

"Tensions have been running high since Stirling."

Holt sat on the bed, a wall torch beside them still burning. Next to that, there was little light in this chamber. The fire was but a smolder now. "And they will continue to do so," he predicted.

Hayden agreed, but that did not mean they needed a mark on their chests proclaiming their family a friend to their northern neighbors. Which was precisely what his cousin was doing even as they sat here, unknowing Edward had brought the hammer down on the Waryn family.

"So we take the Old North Road to Middleton Ridge and part there?"

Haydn squared his shoulders.

"Haydn?"

His brother was to escort Phillipa while he continued north. "We shall see."

He tried to turn around, but Holt didn't let him get that far. His brother grabbed his forearm. "Haydn?" he repeated.

He gave Holt the only answer he had. "I don't know."

"You don't know. . . what precisely?"

"I don't know what we will do at Middleton Ridge." He regained control of his arm but did not turn back around. "Prepare to leave at daybreak."

For a change, Holt didn't say it. But he was surely thinking "do not treat me as a child," something Haydn tried not to do. But he felt protective of his siblings. To him, Holt was still the little boy who tugged on his tunic, asking him to practice swordplay. Or the scamp who followed him and Hugh everywhere, well before he was old enough to carry anything but a blunted wooden sword.

Halfway to his own chamber, where he must reluctantly wake his wife, Haydn froze. The sound was faint at first, but as it grew louder, he could identify it clearly as footsteps. When the steward materialized, his shoulders dropped, relaxing.

"My apologies for startling you, my lord. A servant heard a door and thought you might be awake and needing assistance."

"We will leave at dawn, Master John. It seems the rain has finally ended?" At least, it appeared so from his chamber, though the slits were small and light rain easily could have avoided notice.

"Aye, my lord, it has. Do you care to break your fast in the hall or shall I have the cook pack your party a meal for the road?"

"For the road," he said. "And if you could have my men woken as well."

He nodded. "Aye, my lord. Will that be all?"

Haydn thought back to his and the steward's original conversation. "You mentioned a boon when we arrived. . ."

The steward shook his head. "Nay, my lord. I can not ask it of you. Apologies for—"

"Your hospitality has been most generous. What can I do for you, Master John?"

Something had made the man nervous, and Haydn could only guess it had to do with what he wanted to ask him.

"I hesitate with this request but, as I'm desperate to get her a message. . ." He took a deep breath. "My daughter married a Scot, from the borderlands. Just north of Brockburg."

He immediately understood. And the steward's request was an easy one to fulfill. "You know my family well, then," he mused.

"My daughter's husband," he whispered by way of explanation.

"'Tis no crime to be married to a Scot," Haydn reminded him.

"In these uncertain times. . ." He trailed off.

Haydn thought to reassure him. "I can easily have a message brought to your daughter," he said. Brockburg, the seat of Clan Kerr, was just north across the border from Bristol, where he was headed. His cousins often came to and from both residences. Surely one of them could send a missive quite easily. "I am headed to the border myself," he said.

The man's smile was Haydn's reward for his service. Clearly he worried for his daughter's safety, and on that point, Haydn would not falsely reassure him. Though the corridor between Bristol and Brockburg was relatively safe, courtesy of their two families' alliance, elsewhere along the border was anything but. Even the monthly Day of Truce was proving to be less and less effective now that King Edward had essentially staked a claim in Scotland.

"Thank you, my lord." Master John bowed. "I will prepare the message immediately and see you are sent off with provisions. If you will pardon me, Lord Waryn."

He watched as the steward disappeared down the stair-well and turned toward his chamber. There, in its thresh-old, was his wife. He hadn't heard the door open. Did she do it quietly lest she be heard? Had she been listening the entire time?

"I thought we travelled to Hillstone?"

Haydn wished now, more than ever, they'd had that talk the night before. What could he say? Certainly he wasn't ready to simply trust her to be loyal to him, to his family?

Pushing aside thoughts of their night together, Haydn willed himself to consider his family. The border was dangerous, more now than ever. And they were all in the crosshairs. His aunts and uncles, his cousins. . . .

"Not we, Phillipa. You."

# CHAPTER
# TWENTY

S he spun back inside the chamber, attempting to close the door, but Haydn was too quick. He pushed it open and stepped inside, reaching for her. Phillipa slipped away as her husband closed the door.

Pretending he was not standing just behind her, she walked toward the fire, still roaring as it had last night, courtesy of Haydn no doubt. The same Haydn who was not coming to Hillside Manor.

"I must get to Bristol," he said, coming upon her from behind. When he placed his hand on her arm, she closed her eyes. "Phillipa, look at me."

She could not. He would see the tears that had begun to form in her eyes. Even closing them did not help. Her throat tightened with the implications of his admission, one he'd not shared with her.

"You were to leave me there."

"Phillipa..."

Since she refused to budge, he stepped around her to her front, but still she would not open her eyes. His thumb brushed her cheek, wiping away a single tear that had escaped from under her lashes.

"You could have told me."

Engulfing her in his arms, Haydn didn't deny it. "Aye, I could have."

She felt silly laying her head on the chest of a man who'd just admitted he had planned to abandon her. But it felt so good to be held by him, to breathe in a scent uniquely his. To pretend, for just a moment, they were not one step away from being enemies.

"Where is your primary residence?" she asked without looking up, knowing if she looked at his face, Phillipa would never keep the thin threads of composure she held onto even now. And then she remembered what Lady Kristine had said. "Rymerden Castle," she guessed.

He pulled her closer. "Aye. Just south of Kenshire. The king bequeathed it to my mother as recompense for her father's service, and she passed the title to me."

"And Hillstone Manor?"

"Farther south even. Also a part of my grandfather's holdings which passed to my mother. It is a lovely residence which sits along the North Sea, like Kenshire."

A lovely residence. "You never intended this marriage to be anything but one in name only?"

"I never intended to marry at all." She tried to pull away, but he wouldn't let her. "Phillipa, I wanted to speak to you last eve. *This* is what I wished to discuss. Much has changed between us these past few days. I still must get to Brockburg, but after that. . ." He trailed off.

"Has it changed? We've simply consummated our marriage."

"And that is all? You believe last eve was nothing more than duty? To assure that we are well and truly married?"

"And to produce an heir, of course." She said it only to shield herself from further pain. Of course she thought what they shared was more than that, but Phillipa wasn't fool enough to admit as much.

"If I'd simply wanted to produce an heir, I'd not have asked that we share a chamber, Phillipa. Conceiving a child does not require this."

She'd not been expecting his kiss. But after what she learned, Phillipa wanted to welcome it. Indeed, when his lips touched hers, she gave herself over completely. In an instant, the kiss turned almost desperate. She wanted to believe him. Even if she knew the decision he'd made, to keep them apart, had actually been for the best.

This was where she should tell him everything. What her father had bade her do. Of the king's paranoia and the fact that Haydn's family was, indeed, in danger. She should ask him how they could remain together, in truth, but still protect her sister.

But she did none of that, because Phillipa was certain it wouldn't matter. He said he wanted to talk. But Haydn never denied the fact that he planned for them to live separately or that those plans had changed. Just when she'd found her voice, Phillipa didn't want to use it.

Kissing her husband, being held by him, just felt too good for the dose of reality that would surely lay waste to even an inkling of hope for them as a married couple.

*You believe last eve was nothing more than duty?*

How could she know with what little experience she had? But that he'd asked the question meant maybe, just maybe, Haydn didn't believe it to be true. That last eve was something more. For now, she would enjoy the time they had, that small inkling of hope enough to cling to for this morning, at least, until the sun rose and shined its clari-fying light on the truth of their marriage.

A marriage that balanced as precariously as the very conflict that set the two of them at odds. That declared them enemies when, in truth, no idea could be more false. Unless it was possible to fall in love with your adversary. In which case, Phillipa was well and truly damned.

# TWENTY-ONE

"Once," Holt told Haydn's wife as Haydn's mount navigated around the thick mud that had plagued them all morning, "he challenged a man who'd long earned his spurs to a duel. He was, maybe, ten and two."

"I can hear you easily enough," he called back, riding just in front of them.

Phillipa chuckled. All morning his brother had been telling stories, none of them shedding him in a particularly good light.

"Our brother, Hugh, had to step in. Haydn really wanted to fight the man with his new steel sword."

"What did he do to earn such animosity from a young boy?"

Haydn watched as travellers approached, and now only half listened to his brother's tale. After the attack, he'd been more vigilant than usual. It was not the first skirmish he'd encountered on his travels, nor would it be the last. But he just wished to get them to their destination with no further cause for Phillipa to distress.

She'd had too much of that already. The men, sensing he himself had begun to speak more freely around his wife, did the same. And though his wife also shared stories, some of which were happy, mostly including early memories of her mother or tales of court, nearly all of them were laced with a hesitancy that should not be present when speaking of your family. With each passing moment, he felt more inclined to protect her. More inclined to figure a way out of this mess.

One thing was for certain.

He could not abandon her. Doing so was not in his nature. But neither did he have a clear plan yet. Would he speak freely with her, as one should with their wife? Could he really take her to Bristol Manor?

The horses needed to rest. And Haydn had to speak to his wife.

"We stop there," he said, "before we climb the ridge." Navigating his mount from the road, still watching the approaching party, he waited. "Take the others to the stream," he said to Holt.

"You are not scouting them alone," his brother replied, riding up to him.

"They are but pilgrims," he said, more confident as they approached that there would be no trouble.

"Isaac." Holt nodded to Phillipa. His man understood and began to lead her off the path. His wife looked at him, and then the approaching riding party, before following Isaac. She said nothing, but he could tell Phillipa worried. Likely would do so many times before they reached their destination. But there would be no attack today. No one would be hurt. He said as much to alleviate their fear. "We stay simply to speak to them, to receive word from other travellers. They are holy men," he said.

"Then why do you have Isaac lead me away?"

The wife he'd first met would not have asked the question, and Haydn was glad for it. "Because I am an overly cautious man."

She smiled at him, Haydn returning the gesture, and then rode away with Isaac. Hamon remained, and when Haydn turned back to him and Holt, the two of them were staring at him.

"What is it?" he asked.

Neither answered. But Holt did shake his head.

As the riding party approached, their wagon making slow progress in the mud, he waited for his man to answer.

"You smile as often as your brother today," Hamon said.

"Perhaps he is finally having an influence on me," he quipped.

"Or perhaps it is your wife?" Holt greeted the men first as they passed. "Good day, Father," he said to the priest at the front of the pack. "How goes your journey?"

While the others in his party continued on—stopping to speak to each and every person on the road did not lend itself to arriving at one's destination in a timely manner—the leader walked toward them. Travelling to London on foot was something Haydn didn't envy.

"Well enough, and yours, Lord. . . ?"

"Waryn. And my brother, Sir Holt, and our man, Sir Hamon."

"Greetings, sirs," the priest said. "A warning, of sorts. There is a band of freemen, mercenaries I believe, wreaking havoc as they travel south."

Haydn stopped him. "We encountered their party three days ago."

The priest blinked. Waited. "They were intent on misdeeds," he said, seeming to understand.

"Aye, they were," Haydn agreed. "They attacked us, quite unprovoked. We buried three of them."

The priest crossed himself, said something under his breath that sounded like "God take their souls." Haydn was not sure if those men would be welcomed in heaven, but he kept that thought to himself.

"Any other news from the road?" he asked, aware the man needed to catch up with the others.

"Aye," he said, "although you've likely heard. At Jedburg Abbey word circulated that William Wallace has resurfaced. At first we thought it nothing but a rumor, but the abbot claims to have seen the man himself."

He and Holt exchanged a glance. "You are from the borders, then?" Holt asked.

"We are."

"Did you speak to the abbot yourself?"

"Aye, and he claimed Wallace passed through there for the night with four men. Any news from the south?"

Since the priest was from the border, Haydn could be more candid than he would otherwise. "Other than that the king still licks his wounds and prepares for his next offensive? Nay." He pointed on the path they came from. "Do you know the Fox and Hound?"

"Aye, we stopped briefly yesterday."

"Can we reach it by nightfall, do you believe?"

The priest looked up to the sky and then toward the trees where the path lay ahead. "Mounted? Aye, I do believe so." He smiled, a kindly gesture given they'd confessed to killing two men. "I had best be on my way."

"I trust you find what you look for in London, Father," Holt said.

Since the priest didn't correct him, it seemed that was their final destination after all. "We bid you a good eve and safe travel, Father," Haydn added, knowing the man must be on his way.

"I will pray for you, Lord Waryn. Many thanks for keeping the passage safe."

Haydn nodded, surprised. So he knew of him, after all. "Bless you, Father," Hamon added as the man wandered away.

"The passage?" Hamon asked as they rode to join Phillipa and Isaac.

"I've heard it before," he said, spying his wife. "Some use the term for the borderlands between Bristol and Brockburg."

"Breac made mention of it when I saw him last." Holt dismounted first, before they reached the others. Phillipa bent down to the stream while Isaac finished tying off his mount. "He said as more learned of it, the path would be more and more difficult to keep stable."

"Indeed." Haydn dismounted as well. "Take this?" he asked Holt, anxious to speak to Phillipa. "We rest the horses and leave," he looked at the sun, "at sext." They'd gotten an earlier start, and he was pleased with the time they'd made. By midday, though, their party would need to be well on their way to reach the Fox and Hound.

"We reach Middleton Ridge in two days' time," Holt called to him as Haydn walked down the grassy slope toward his wife. His brother's meaning was clear. *You have two days to decide where to go next.* Would he continue north with Hamon, as planned, Holt and Isaac escorting Phillipa to Hillstone? Or would their plans be altered?

"The water is so cold," she said, standing, shaking her hands dry.

"And will grow even colder the farther north we get," he

said, grabbing her hand and leading Phillipa away from prying eyes. He could wait no longer. When they were hidden from view, the thicket serving as a barrier between them and the men, he pressed her to a thick tree and crashed his lips to hers. Phillipa welcomed him instantly, opening for him. He deepened the kiss, their tongues tangling as if they were well acquainted by now. She wore a simple travelling gown Master John had insisted she take, as the one she'd arrived at Caldwell Manor wearing had been muddied and beyond repair. It had been left by a countess who'd passed through. She'd taken too many trunks with her through the muddy marshes and her companions were all too pleased to leave some of them behind.

Its neckline was lower than her own, a fact Haydn took advantage of now. His lips trailed from hers down her neck to the opening in her gown. Rubbing his thumbs over both peaks as he did so, Haydn was pleased when his wife grabbed a fistful of his hair, preventing him from lifting his head.

He teased and licked and pressed himself into her as Phillipa circled her hips. "Please, Haydn," she breathed. He did not hesitate. Freeing himself with one hand and lifting her gown and shift both with the other, he raised his head, watching as she realized what they were about to do.

"If someone comes. . ."

"They will not."

He wished he could see under her gown, the sight of his wife's garter and hose something he'd been imagining all morn.

It was all he could do, apparently. Think of his wife in various states of undress. But now, as he entered her despite the layers of clothing separating them, he did not have to imagine any longer. Once fully inside her, Haydn kept his hand there. They must be quick about it, as much as he'd like to linger here, in this very position, all day.

She held onto him as Haydn eased his way in, and out. When he circled his thumb and Phillipa nearly cried out, he captured the sound with his lips. Attempting to erase the pain he'd caused her thus far, Haydn took her more deeply.

He silently begged for her to find pleasure, both as an apology and a promise. They would talk this night. Would form a plan together. Could he trust his wife fully? Nay. But neither did he wish to leave her.

"Mmm," she moaned against his lips. Squeezing his shoulders, Phillipa was close to release. As was he. In fact, so close, he wondered how he could hang on much longer.

He couldn't.

"Phillipa." He broke the kiss, pumping into her harder and harder, his wife taking every bit of him with a vigor he never could have imagined she possessed. "Come with me."

Sure enough, she did. Squeezing him, Phillipa found her release as he cried out, unable to hold back. The sight of her this way, wildly abandoned in the middle of the woods with nothing but trees and thicket as their witness. . . he would remember this moment for the rest of his life as the one when he realized he was in love with his wife. This was no ordinary coupling. Every time they were together he felt closer, more connected to her, than anyone else in the world.

"Phillipa," he breathed, pulling his hand away. "You are mine."

That was not what he'd meant to say. But the possessiveness he felt for her was all-consuming. Even now she could carry his child. And if she did not, she would one day.

But he did not say the words. Something held him back. And unfortunately, Haydn knew what that something was. He desired his wife. Had fallen in love with her in such a short span of time he'd call another man a fool for claiming it.

But did he trust her?

# CHAPTER
# TWENTY-TWO

To my lord, Robert Pernell, 6th Earl of Sherfield, my most venerable father,

    *My deepest regret is that I've had naught opportunity to write to you before now. Our journey is but halfway ended and already we've endured an attack, through which I found safety and protection from my husband and his men.*

    *Poor weather delayed us further, and this eve, I write by the light of a lone candle in the Fox and Hound, an inn of sorts. There is no town or village nearby with which to establish my location, but I thought to share with you what I've learned thus far, as was your directive.*

"You are still awake?"

Having heard the door open, she folded the parchment in half and turned toward the door.

"Should I not be?" she asked as Haydn walked toward her. He glanced at the small desk, and the missive she'd been writing, but said nothing about it.

"I've become accustomed to you falling asleep on me," he said, kissing her on the forehead and sitting on the bed.

Such a small, simple gesture, but one that seemed impossible a sennight ago.

"Amice warned me the journey would be long. I had no notion, truly. I've not been farther than from my home to court and back."

Haydn unsheathed his sword and laid it on the only other table in the bedchamber, which, according to the innkeeper, was the largest of them. She would not wish to see a small one.

"Has she travelled far then, your maid?"

Phillipa chuckled. "Nay. But she often offers counsel on matters with which she has little experience."

"Like my sister. Haddie seems to know all, even more so than my brothers or I, or even our parents."

"Tell me of her. Your sister."

Haydn began to unlace his boots. "She is a younger version of our mother. Strong-willed, determined, obstinate even, though she'd certainly deny it."

"They both sound lovely."

"Ha! Lovely. 'Tis not the first word that comes to mind." He smiled, removing the second boot. "I jest, of course. Haddie is also good, and kind, like my mother. They are both remarkable women." Phillipa sat back, content to listen to him. "My mother held Kenshire Castle on her own when her cousin attempted to wrest it from her after my grandfather died. She was betrothed to the Earl of Archbald at the time."

"Archbald?" She knew the man, and his sons. "His wife died many years ago."

"I've heard the same, but have no occasion to meet him. After she fell in love with my father, she cleverly gave much of her property back to the king as recompense to break the betrothal."

"And he agreed to it?"

Haydn stood back up and came to her. As always when he looked at her that way, Phillipa's heart began to race. "He did."

When he stopped just short of the desk, his gaze edging toward the missive, his expression changed. She looked between him and the folded parchment.

"'Tis a letter," she said by way of explanation.

"To your sister?"

Would that it was to Catherine. "Nay." She looked up. "To my father."

His lips tightened. "He asked that you write to him."

"I'd not do so otherwise." Phillipa stood up. "I believe it is time for that discussion," she said, knowing it would be a difficult one but also that if they were to have a chance at any semblance of a real marriage, she could not bear the burden of keeping her sister safe alone. She reached out to touch him, but Haydn spun away from her too quickly. He moved back toward the bed, ran his hands through the hair she'd gripped just that afternoon, and said naught. "You know this already, Haydn. 'Tis why we were married."

When he turned back around, it wasn't the Haydn that she'd made love to earlier. Or the one that had begun to share more of himself. Instead it was the one who had not spoken to her on their wedding day.

"So that you might spy on me. And my family." His voice was flat. Emotionless.

"Spy? Would that not imply you knew nothing of my intentions? I never lied to you, Haydn."

"What do you write to him?"

She grabbed the missive. "Read it. What do you think it contains?"

He shrugged. "I can not guess," he said, not moving toward her, or the letter.

"Do you believe I would betray you after what's passed between us?"

"Would you not? It would be noble of you, by his standards. And the king's."

"Noble is also protecting my sister despite what I might want." There it was. She said it. What Haydn would do with the information, she could not guess.

He paused and frowned. "It is as I thought. And if I were you, I'd do anything to protect her."

"You are angry."

"Aye, I am angry. You write a letter to your father telling him. . ." He shrugged. "All you've learned, perhaps?"

"All I've learned? You share so little of yourself, what do you believe I could possibly say to him?"

His eyes narrowed. "I could see you, Phillipa, through the fabric of the tent. When you leaned forward as we spoke of Bristol and my cousin Rory."

She thought back to that night. "I was curious—"

"Only when talk turned to my relative who just happened to live at the border."

Phillipa could not remember the specifics of their discussion, but she had wondered since what Rory might be involved in. But Haydn looked at her with such suspicion, as if all along she'd done nothing but vie for information. And nothing could be further from the truth. She didn't *want* to know. Not any longer.

"If you so mistrust me, then why not just have me escorted to Hillside as you planned?" Phillipa could not resist lashing out now. He was supposed to be the one to help her through this, but instead, he pushed her away.

"Perhaps I will," he shot back.

Taking a deep breath, she tried to calm both of their tempers. "Haydn, truly, I know nothing of significance. And if I did. . ." Her voice trailed off.

"If you did?" The suspicion in his eyes told her more than Haydn's words about what the outcome of this discussion would be. "If you knew the whereabouts of Wallace, for instance?"

Wallace. There was no one the king despised more. "Do you know where he is?"

"If I did, could I trust you with the information or would you put it in that letter?"

"What concern of yours would it be? You are English too, Haydn. Wallace was responsible for many deaths at Stirling and—"

"I am a borderer," he interrupted, his voice harsh. "And a Waryn. Kin to Clan Kerr."

And at least some of his family fought with Wallace. He didn't have to say it. Which meant the king had good reason to question the Earl of Kenshire and his family's loyalty.

*But what of Catherine? What of me?*

"'Tis complicated," she admitted.

"Nay." Haydn sat on the bed and slipped his boots back on. He was leaving. She wanted to say something to make him stay, but what could Phillipa say that would make him trust her? Precisely nothing. To him, she would always be the daughter of the king's advisor first, Phillipa, his wife, second. "'Tis not complicated at all," he said, more to himself than to her. Then grabbing his belt and sword, Haydn walked out of their small chamber without another word and closed the door behind him.

# CHAPTER
# TWENTY-THREE

They'd not spoken all morn.

Holt and the men knew better than to approach him. They knew he hadn't slept with Phillipa courtesy of the stablehand who'd asked if he'd gotten any sleep in the stable loft on account of ol' Ned neighing during the night. Not that he'd intended to hide the fact. As they approached the fork in the road that marked the climb to Middleton Ridge due north and the road that would lead them northeast, toward Hillstone Manor, it would become apparent enough that he and his wife would be parting ways.

Haydn had hardly slept the night before, a fact that helped to lend him little patience when his brother did ride ahead to join him.

"What is the plan?"

"You know the plan, Holt."

His brother had asked that morn if he still intended on the original plan or if he would be accompanying him to Bristol Manor. Haydn had told him then, and repeated himself now. "You and Isaac are to escort Phillipa to Hillstone Manor and then head to Kenshire to tell them the deed is done."

"The deed." Holt was definitely not going to let this one go. "Phillipa is a 'deed' now?"

A hawk's cry drew their attention. Haydn watched him soar, the sky blue and cloudless today. At least the weather was with them. "What do you want me to say, Holt?"

His brother's characteristic grin was nowhere to be found. "I want you to tell me what happened. I thought things were different between you."

Haydn had thought so too. Despite himself, he glanced back, but Phillipa was with the men around the bend so he could hear, but not see, them. "She was writing a letter," he ground out, knowing Holt would not rest until he explained. "A letter to her father, that he bade her send, reporting on what she knows."

That quieted his brother. For a time at least. The road, paved in places with stone, afforded them an easier ride but more opportunity for trouble. As a merchant approached, Haydn nodded in greeting. The man sat at the front of his wagon with a young boy as his companion. A son, no doubt.

He ignored the pang in his chest at the thought that Phillipa could, even now, be carrying their child. One he would gladly welcome but who would grow up very differently than he and his siblings. Cursing King Edward, a daily ritual now, he slowed his mount, waiting for the merchant to pass the others. When the wagon creaked by Phillipa and the men without incident, Haydn spun in his saddle and rode forward.

But not before seeing her. Phillipa looked precisely how he felt.

"What did she tell him?" Holt asked as they rode forward once again.

He paused. "I didn't see the letter," Haydn admitted.

"You didn't see it?"

He stared straight ahead. "No."

"What did she say was in the letter?"

Haydn did not want to do this. "Holt, she admitted her father asked her to write. He and the king hold her sister's future as collateral. What do you think was in there?" Thankfully they'd been careful not to reveal much. She didn't know about Rory or, Lord forbid it, Galien. Uncle Torr's son would be the first to be arrested with Wallace if the man was still indeed lurking around the borders.

"Do you truly believe Sherfield would sabotage his daughter's future to punish Phillipa?"

He didn't hesitate. "I do."

"To be clear, brother, your wife did not admit to sending sensitive information to her father."

"Nay, she did not."

"But you would condemn her as if she'd done so?"

He was going to say this once, and once only. "She was writing a letter. To her father, the closest advisor to King Edward at present and a man who cares nothing for his own offspring. Influence. Money. Power. Yes. Phillipa and Catherine? Nay. We never had a chance. So leave off, Holt."

Riding ahead, Haydn prayed his brother would not join him. After a time, it became clear he was alone with his own thoughts. He only stopped when the very place he'd been dreading came into view. An old granite obelisk marked the spot where the two roads diverged.

Halting, Haydn turned to wait for the others. As they joined him, there was only one face he watched. She did not

shy away from staring straight at him but, as she'd done in
the beginning, Phillipa said nothing.

Haydn wanted her to rail at him. To insist that she
would never betray him, or his family. To refuse to go to
Hillstone, indignant at the very idea. Instead, resigned, she
waited for him to give her and the men instructions.

And so he did.

"This is where we part ways. Holt and Isaac will escort
you to Hillside Manor, my lady. Your lady's maid and
belongings should provide some measure of comfort, and
Holt will introduce you to the staff there." Even to his own
ears, the words, though kindly stated, sounded harsh.
Disconnected.

Her chin lifted, but still, his beautiful, passionate wife
said nothing. So he turned to Holt.

"Keep her safe, brother. Godspeed. I shall see you at
Kenshire."

He'd been witness to many deaths, both in battle, and
in his own family. Kenshire's steward, Peter, who he'd loved
like a second father. His uncle. Too many others, gone too
soon. But not once had Haydn shed a tear. He had never
witnessed his father crying and so he assumed he should
never do so either.

Which was why, as he rode away after one last look at
her face, Haydn was so surprised to feel his throat tighten.
He squeezed his eyes shut, thankful Hamon was behind
him. Regaining control, he took a series of deep breaths,
vowing not to play the vision of her stricken expression
over and over in his mind. Instead, he replaced it with a
vision of his mother in their garden at Kenshire. With
Haddie standing atop the wall walk, watching waves crash
onto the shore in the distance. With he and Hugh jesting

good-naturedly in the training yard. Of his father and he and Holt hunting.

They would not lose Kenshire to the king's whims. Bristol Manor and its inhabitants would not be targeted for housing traitors. The passage would remain open and safe, despite the war raging around them.

For that to happen, Haydn just needed to forget that he loved his wife.

# CHAPTER
# TWENTY-FOUR

wo days after Haydn had left, Phillipa sat with Holt for a supper of pigeon stew. The inn was larger than most others they'd stayed at on their journey. When they arrived in the small village of Crenshire, Phillipa had not expected much. But apparently the inn was known for miles, its owner the fourth son of a baron who had coin to spare and no other property inheritance to speak of. The hall could have been one in a manor house or even a small castle.

The stew was surprisingly delicious.

"Was Isaac able to find the ferrier?" she asked.

"Nay. He's attempting to speak to the blacksmith even though his shop is closed for the evening. If necessary, the shoe could wait until Hillstone for repair."

They spoke of the weather. Of his horse's sprung shoe. Of the journey ahead. But never of Haydn. It took some time after he rode away from Phillipa to reconcile that she had, indeed, been well and truly abandoned by her husband. And not for a short period of time. According to

Holt, he rarely visited Hillstone. It was the only question she'd asked in regards to her husband.

"Where will you go after Hillstone?" she asked, pushing away the bowl of stew. Though it was quite good, Phillipa could not eat another spoonful. "Apologies," she added before he could answer. "I did not mean to pry."

Holt leveled a look at her that very much reminded her of Haydn. It was the kind of disapproval he showed whenever she refused to speak her mind. Despite everything, Phillipa still wished to meet the Countess of Kenshire one day. She must be a most remarkable woman to have raised such men.

"I am not Haydn," he said. Holt sat back in the chair, watching for her reaction. There had been an understanding of sorts, that they would not speak of his brother.

Her husband.

"You are not worried I will learn something untoward? That I shall race to my room to put the words to parchment to send to my father?"

Holt studied her. He looked into her eyes for such a long time Phillipa had the urge to look away. Instead, she held his gaze.

"Nay," he said finally. "I am not."

Nothing that he said could have surprised her more. "You are not?"

Holt grabbed his mug of ale. "Nay."

What could she say to that? "Then you are of a different opinion than your brother."

Finishing a swig of ale, he ignored the barmaid who attempted to flirt with him as she walked past their table. To others it must appear as if she and Holt were husband and wife. And yet the maid did not seem to let the fact interrupt her flirting.

He sighed. "Haydn lives in the shadow of our father."

"I'm sorry?" Surely she didn't understand.

"We all do. But Haydn more than Hugh or I. As the oldest, I suppose." He shook his head, seeing her face. "My father is not to blame. He is simply. . . there is no comparison to him. And the love he and our mother share. . ." Holt shrugged. "Haydn is deserving of the same kind of love."

At first she thought Holt meant that 'twas her fault he would not have it. But the corner of his lips tugged up in a sort of sad smile, not one which was accusatory. Just resigned.

"I've not met your father, of course. But I could not imagine he is more of a man than Haydn. No disrespect to him, of course. But your brother. . . ." She sighed.

"My brother?"

What could she say? Phillipa had been so angry with him when he rode away. But today, she was just as angry at herself. She should have spoken when she remained silent. Fought for him. But she didn't because, well, Haydn was right. They'd been doomed from the day their marriage was conceived as a way for the king to keep the Waryn family in check.

"Phillipa?"

"Your brother. . ." She watched as the serving maid strained her neck to see Holt from the table she was serving. She chuckled, looking back to Holt. "'Tis just the maid," she whispered. "She nearly toppled herself looking this way."

"The one with red hair piled atop her head?"

She startled. "Aye, but I did not think you noticed her."

"I notice everything," he said, more serious than she'd become accustomed to from him. His easy manner hid an intelligence, she thought. If Phillipa guessed correctly, there was more to Holt than he let others believe. "Your brother," she continued, "is the kind of man women dream of taking as their husband. Strong and able. He's quick-witted," she said, "and loyal."

"His head is harder than a block of iron though." Holt took another swig and turned toward the maid. They both laughed when she nearly dropped a wooden tray of stew and bread.

"You distract her."

"She is easily distracted," he said. But now Phillipa knew that look. Before, she'd not have understood completely. Some women were likely unlucky enough never to truly understand, as would have been her fate if she'd married most of the prospects that had tried to claim her hand.

Instead, she was married to a man that had showed her a passion she'd never be able to explore. Was it better, she wondered, not to have known it all? It would have been easier that way, certainly.

"You are in love with Haydn," Holt said suddenly.

In response, she reached into the folds of the mantle that now sat beside her. Gripping the parchment, knowing what it represented, how things might change once she finished it and found a messenger to take it to her father, Phillipa paused. And then looked into the eyes of a man that was like a younger version of the one she loved.

She'd made the only decision she could. And Phillipa would not back away from it.

As she pulled it from the folds, the corner of her letter caught on a bit of wool. She tugged at it, setting it free, and then slid it across the table to her brother-in-law. No words were needed. He would understand soon enough.

# CHAPTER
# TWENTY-FIVE

B uilt on a river basin just two days' ride south of the border, Bristol Manor was once nothing more than a single defense tower with an attached hall. Surrounded by a curtain wall, an addition his grandfather made before it was captured by Clan Kerr, it now included a solar block, storerooms, and a stable. A handsome and well-fortified structure, though not as vast as Kenshire Castle.

Not surprisingly, he didn't make it to the stable when his cousin approached. Before he even reached the gatehouse, the guards knew he'd been coming. Glad to see Rory was here—he'd been worried since the priest made mention of Wallace—he immediately dismounted. Handing a stablehand his reins, he embraced his cousin, only letting go when Rory slapped him on the arse as he often did to everyone.

Men. Women. Family. Strangers. Rory was his uncle Bryce through and through. Although Haydn had never actually seen his uncle do that.

"You will get yourself into trouble putting your hands where they don't belong."

Rory, as always, was unapologetic. "I've found my hands get me out of trouble more than into it."

Haydn shook his head, looking around the courtyard. Arriving so late, well after sundown, it was a quieter scene than usual.

"Surely you don't travel alone?" Rory asked.

They walked past the well toward the front entrance of the manor.

"I have one man with me. He is speaking with one of the guards and should be along soon."

Although the resemblance wasn't as strong as with Haydn and his brothers, he and Rory shared the same black Waryn hair and blue eyes. And while some did mistake them for brothers, Haydn thought Hugh looked more like his cousin than any of them.

"'Tis good to see you, cousin," he said in earnest. "I worried with all that has been happening."

Usually Rory would brush off his concern. That he did not was telling. Haydn held out a hand to stop him before they entered the keep. He liked less the look Rory gave him now. Something was afoot, and he sensed the danger was close to home.

"Tell me," Haydn said. As always, her face intruded on his thoughts. It shouldn't. Not now. Not when he, finally, had something to distract him. For there was no doubt it was worry etched on his cousin's face.

"Galien is within."

That alone should not be cause for concern. Instead, a visit from their Scots cousin would be, if not for one simple fact.

Wallace had been spotted in England.

He thought it must have been a rumor. Even when the priest claimed to have seen him, Haydn had been skeptical. But that fact, coupled with Galien being at Bristol, had the hair on his arms standing straight. It was a good thing he'd come so quickly.

"Haydn!" a female voice called. They had just barely entered the hall when he was nearly tackled. Aside from his mother and Haddie, his cousin Rylee was his favorite female in all of England.

*Stop. Thinking. Of Phillipa.*

"'Tis good to see you," he said as Rylee's arms went around him. By now the servants were accustomed to the show of affection that he knew was not very common. Especially in a place as public as the hall. Supper had ended, it seemed, but at least ten or so people lingered.

"Where are your parents?"

"Mother had a headache," Rory said, his sister laughing at the way he said it. It was common knowledge that Aunt Catrina's headaches were anything but, and Haydn loved to tease his cousins about it.

"She is still getting those, aye?"

"Ugh." Rylee slapped him on the arm. "Would you care for me to speak about your parents thus?"

In fact, he would not. So Haydn smartly said not another word. Instead he let himself be led to a table in the hall after handing his mantle to a servant. A chess board had been abandoned on the table. "I disturbed your game," he guessed as his cousins sat down. He waved to those he knew, thanked a servant who promised to bring him a meal, and sat down alongside his cousins.

"You did nothing of the sort," Rory said.

With a quick look at the board, he realized Rory must be on the losing side. Rylee confirmed it.

"Saved by Haydn's arrival," she said.

He was about to sit when he noticed someone walking toward them. Haydn waited until Galien was upon them and embraced him as he did the others. Galien Kerr was taller than most, except perhaps his father. The chief's son looked like Haydn's uncle Toren too. With brown hair to his shoulders, the man was an intimidating figure, and Haydn was glad to call him family rather than foe.

"A family reunion of sorts," he said as Galien joined them. "I didn't know who I'd find here." A simple meal of roasted chicken and warm bread was placed in front of him.

"My apologies, Lord Waryn," the serving girl said. He didn't recognize her but she clearly knew him. She was pretty. At least, he'd have thought so once. Now there was just one woman whom he wished was standing beside him instead. "It was all the cook could manage—"

"No apologies necessary, thank you," he said, dismissing her.

"Sit," Rylee said. "Tell us why you are here."

He wanted to ask the same of Galien but refrained. That was not a discussion for the hall where others were present.

"I'm afraid this is not merely a social call."

"When is it ever?" Galien asked. One spring, Galien had been visiting Kenshire Castle when he heard a female servant say Galien's voice was like walking so deep into the forest you could not see. An unusual description, but one he understood easily. It was just one of the reasons everyone gathered when Galien spoke. He could make waking up in the morning sound like a grand adventure if that was a tale he chose to tell.

"These days?" he asked, wondering the same of his Scots cousin. "We've much to discuss," he told them. "But not here." Galien and Rory exchanged a glance that confirmed something was, indeed, afoot. He took a bite of bread, which was still warm.

"What can you tell us about your visit?" Rylee asked.

"Well," he said, chasing the bread with a swig of ale and pretending to think. "Ahh, yes. There is the small matter of my wedding."

Rory nearly spit out his ale. "Pardon? I thought you said 'wedding.'"

He tore off a piece of the chicken in front of him. "I did," he said, popping it into his mouth and enjoying his cousins' expressions.

"You are. . . married?" Rory asked, appalled, which earned a harsh look from his sister.

"I am." He lowered his voice, though it would be common knowledge soon enough. "To the Earl of Sherfield's daughter." If he thought to shock them with news of his marriage, the name of his bride left them all gaping. Despite what little joy was left in him, Haydn laughed, ignoring the pang in his chest at the thought of Phillipa. "As I said, we have much to discuss."

# TWENTY-SIX

I t was just him and Galien as Rory shut the door behind him. Rylee had gone to bed long ago, but despite the hour, and his travels, Haydn was not tired. He'd drunk enough ale to fill a barrel, and Galien wasn't far behind.

"A pair of us," his cousin said, his accent not as thick as some Scots but noticeable all the same. They sat comfortably in a solar chamber on the ground floor of the manor, behind the hall. Despite the size of the manor, the solar was as large as Kenshire's, built for discussions such as this one. Haydn stared into the fire as if it would help to solve the many problems they now faced.

"Aye," he agreed. "Though I'd not trade places with you, Galien. You've a target on your back that grows larger each day."

They all knew Galien fought for Wallace, as had other of his cousins and members of their clan. But with Uncle Toren never officially or openly declaring for him, or Comyn or Bruce, Kerr loyalties remained firmly to themselves alone, as it was with many of the border clans.

"We all do," he agreed. "Though if Umphraville can survive, so can we." No one changed sides between the English and Scottish more than the newly elected Guardian of Scotland. "Umphraville also does not have an English family to protect."

Galien narrowed his eyes. "No reminders of our duty are necessary, cousin."

"'Tis not a reminder but a fact. He stands to lose holdings in England, but nothing more."

"No one knows how precarious our position more than I."

The two men fell silent, Haydn not saying what he was thinking. That his cousin continued to train with Wallace, as he'd admitted to this night, meant Galien did not really understand how precarious their position was at all.

"I am married." He rose from his chair, reached for the tankard, and poured another ale, first for himself and then for Galien. "Married," he repeated, sitting back down. "To the Earl of Sherfield's daughter."

The corners of Galien's lips tugged upward. "I take it back."

"As you should." Haydn watched his cousin drink, waiting for him to, perhaps, concede to what Haydn had been saying all eve. Now was the time to regroup. To let Comyn and Bruce take up the cause. To go back to Brockburg for a spell.

Galien made a sound of disgust. "They are as like to line their pockets with English coin than help wrest Scotland from Edward's grip."

"And you are as like to get yourself killed than find freedom from a man who destroyed Wallace at Falkirk and itches to do it again."

A grunt was the only response he got from Galien.

"You are your father's son," Haydn said.

"If there is a man more like his own father than you, I do not know him."

"There will never be another Geoffrey Waryn," he said, in earnest.

"There is already. He sits before me."

Haydn looked up, thinking his cousin jesting. But he did not appear to be at all. "Then you do not truly know my father."

"Aye, Haydn. I know him well. A protector. A fighter. A man who loves his family above all with friends who would lay down their swords for him at a moment's notice. I am well acquainted with Uncle Geoffrey. And with his eldest son."

"You forgot husband, his greatest achievement of all, according to him."

"I did not forget it," Galien said. "I merely listed the qualities you have in common with him. You are nay a husband in truth to your wife."

Leave it to Galien to both offer the greatest praise and deepest cut in one breath. "I would be, if I could."

"Aye?"

He took a long sip of ale. "Aye."

"It seems to me you care deeply for a woman whose only crime was trying to protect her sister." He'd told his cousin of his wife's predicament.

"You sound like Holt," he said.

"Your baby brother is wiser than he lets on," Galien said, echoing his own thoughts. It was difficult to take Holt seriously, but more often than not, his brother was on target with his thinking. In this, however, Haydn did not trust him. Nor did he trust himself. "I refuse to let my feelings for my wife endanger our family."

Galien leaned forward, forcing Haydn's attention. "Nothing is without risk." He raised his goblet. "Nothing worth having, that is."

# TWENTY-SEVEN

"How many more days, do you think, until we reach Hillstone?" Weary from travel, more than prepared to bed down for the night, in a bed not made from straw, Phillipa looked up at the sign.

It was the first time they'd been in an actual town. And judging from the size of the inn, it would be her best chance to actually fulfill that very simple dream. Before marrying Haydn, she'd never attended to herself, much less slept on a mattress filled with straw. Or a bedroll as she'd done three nights now on this journey.

But she was alive, had not been abused by her new husband, and had a plan to keep Catherine safe. So Phillipa had no complaints that were of any significance. She missed her husband, despite the fact that he had abandoned her. She woke in the night attempting, unsuccessfully, to forget dreams of him that, at times, felt as if they were real.

"Less than a sennight," Holt said.

"I will take the horses," Isaac said as she dismounted.

The sun had already set, yet townspeople still went about their business. The street was paved, cobblestones beneath their feet keeping the mud and dirt at bay. Holt had told her the town was relatively new, having just received its charter the year before. It seemed to have built up quickly in that time. Stray pigs roamed the street, merchants and servants made their way to and fro, and Phillipa even spied a group of what appeared to be noblemen at the end of the block.

When the curfew bell sounded as they walked toward the inn's doors, an urgency could be felt that wasn't there before. Smiths. Brewers. They would all stop their work and none would be found on the streets without lanterns soon.

"Oh." She froze on the threshold. Phillipa had not been expecting such a grand hall. It was unlike any of the inns in which they'd stayed thus far. Larger, and certainly more lively. There seemed to be people everywhere. "It did not look so large from the street."

Holt strained his neck to look both ways beyond her. "I thought as much. The guilds are closely associated here, and it seems as if the tavern next door and the inn have combined."

She realized as they entered he was right. Where there once must have been a wall, now tall wooden beams remained between what seemed to be two separate halls. There was even a troubadour in one corner reciting words she could not hear.

"The owner must be wealthy to hire such a man." Even she knew they came at a considerable cost, typically reserved for nobles.

"The baron is likely not in residence."

She'd seen a fortified manor house in the distance as they rode into town, but she did not understand the connection. "The baron?"

"Aye. Entertainers such as he would offer their services at a reduced cost until the lord returns. Rather than spend their time traveling to a new town."

She was about to ask who the baron was when they were interrupted by a woman. She was short, plump, and by her smile, seemingly a kindly woman. "My lord." She bowed. "My lady. Can I offer you a meal?"

At first Phillipa thought her a serving woman, but as she looked closer at her kirtle, she could see the material was quite fine indeed. So when she introduced herself as the owner of the inn, Phillipa was less taken aback. But still surprised the owner was a woman. To her knowledge, such an occurrence was not common.

As she and Holt negotiated lodgings and a meal, Phillipa spied Isaac walking toward them. "Would it be possible," she asked, "to take my meal abovestairs? I would very much like to rest." She nodded to Isaac. "And will leave the two of you to your pleasures." Of which there seemed to be plenty. Gaming, music, women. . . the men could do to be alone, and Phillipa would be content to change out of her gown.

"Shall I send a bath along with your meal, my lady?"

"If such a thing is possible, I would be grateful."

Though the men protested, Phillipa was overjoyed to find herself, some time later, in a comfortably sized room sitting in hot water for the first time in days. Phillipa laid her head back on the side of the wooden tub, memories of another, much larger one taking hold. Usually she forced her mind elsewhere, but tonight, she wanted to remember.

She could almost feel his hands on her. An ache in her chest left her hollow, the loss, unbearable. Damn him. Opening her eyes, she reluctantly washed and stepped out of the tub. Drying her wet hair as best she could, Phillipa moved to the small trunk that the packhorse so kindly, even if unwillingly, carried each day. She pulled out the brush and ran it through her hair, tears springing to her eyes so suddenly Phillipa had no recourse but to let them flow.

She missed him. With every waking breath, she missed him. And even though she had a plan, some small hope that they could be together, even Holt admitted it could be weeks, or months, before he came to Hillstone. When he did, Phillipa would not hold back. First, she would tell him what she thought of him leaving. And then, she would kiss him so thoroughly he'd regret riding away that day. And maybe, just maybe, he would let her in.

Let her love him.

She jumped at the sound of a knock on her door. Holt would not disturb her now, and it was too soon for them to come for the tub. Phillipa had intended to remain in it much longer, but the memories of another bath lessened the enjoyment she'd thought she would feel in it.

"Who is there?" she called, having been careful to lock the door behind her.

"I've your meal, Lady Waryn," a maid called from the other side. She turned the lock and let her into the chamber.

"Thank you," she said as the young girl placed a wooden tray on the sole small table, which served that very purpose. The girl bowed and looked to the tub. "I will send someone to have it removed. Good even, my lady."

"Good eve," she replied, walking her to the door. When she stepped through it, Phillipa pushed it closed. But just before it did so, the door stuck on something. She pushed it harder, but it refused to budge. Stepping forward, she meant to locate the obstacle and gasped.

It could not be.

CHAPTER
# TWENTY-EIGHT

He was starved for her.

Haydn hadn't realized how much he'd truly missed her until now, He'd planned this moment so many times on the journey. At first, he thought to find her at Hillstone. But pushing himself, and Hamon, riding well into the night most days, he'd picked up their trail. And when he realized he was getting closer, that he might find her on the road, Haydn pushed even harder. It became apparent that morn he would catch them as long as he arrived in town before daybreak.

Haydn knew his brother would come here, so he'd not been surprised to see he and Isaac in the hall. But when he did not see Phillipa, Haydn knew a moment of panic like never before. Thankfully Holt was quick to tell him she simply wished to rest. Tomorrow he'd deal with his brother's obvious disapproval of him.

But right now, he cared for only one person's forgiveness.

He had meant to say he was sorry. Instead, Haydn pushed his way inside, slammed the door, and pulled his wife toward him. His mouth sought hers, and found it. Their kiss was unlike any other they had shared. He kissed her to say he was sorry. To say he loved her. To say he wanted to be with her more than anything else in the world.

Their tongues slashed, Haydn not even realizing he'd slipped off her shift until his hands found the treasure beneath. He cupped her breasts, pinching her nipples between his fingers. In response, Phillipa tugged on his shirt, so he broke contact only long enough to undress more quickly than he had in his whole life.

They said nothing. Haydn had too many words, and Phillipa, for her part, still appeared stunned to see him. Undressed, he pulled her back, never intending to let go.

"Wrap your legs around me," he said, lifting his wife, who did just that. Kissing her thoroughly on the way to the bed, he reluctantly broke contact and instantly missed the touch of her skin on his. Not wanting to be without it, he climbed over her and did not hesitate.

Ensuring she was ready for him and spreading her legs, Haydn buried himself deep. He cried out, as did she, as he thrust into her. Again and again, watching her, but saying nothing. Reaching between them, he used his thumb, circling it, wanting to hear his wife scream in release. Wanting her to feel as uncontrolled as he was at this moment.

Nothing, including the goddamn king of England himself, could stop them.

Never taking his eyes from her, Haydn lowered himself, his hand still between them. When he claimed her mouth once more, mimicking each and every thrust with his tongue, Phillipa squeezed his shoulders, her nails digging into him.

Haydn welcomed it. The pain he'd caused her, caused them both. . . she could rake her nails down his back, drawing blood, and he would let her. Gladly. She may have already done so. As she cried out, Haydn did not wait another moment to find his own release as well.

Collapsing on her, when he was finally able to find his breath, Haydn's heart beating so loudly that surely his wife could hear it, he raised his head. "Hello, Phillipa."

"Hello, Haydn."

Reluctantly pulling from her and dropping beside his wife on the bed, Haydn propped his head in his hand and pulled a strand of wet hair from her face. His eyes darted to the bathtub and then back to her. "How was your bath?"

She watched him warily. "Boring."

His laughter seemed to lighten the mood between them. How he'd missed that smile. And ever thought he could stay away from her. What had he been thinking?

"I am sorry," he said, "for leaving."

Phillipa shivered, so Haydn repositioned himself, pushing the coverlet down and then back over them. Unfortunately she brought it up high enough that her breasts were now covered too. 'Twas well enough. He'd not be able to focus otherwise.

"Haydn—"

"Wait, let me start. We will think of a way to keep your sister safe. We must. Because I can not be without you for any day. I was raised by two parents who love each other so dearly, none of us ever hoped to find the same. But I think, deep inside, it's why I've found one reason or another to reject every match my parents had suggested. I wanted what they had and never thought to find it. Certainly not with the daughter of a man who has the power to destroy my family. Or at least, try to do so. But I will not let him. If we have to fight, we fight. The borderers know little peace and have fought for as many years as I am alive. Never the king of England himself, but so be it. I was a coward, afraid of loving you."

"Or maybe afraid you were not worthy of it."

A lump formed in his throat. She knew him better than she should, given the amount of time they'd known each other. "Aye. Or that precisely."

"I do love you, Phillipa. We will find a path forward, together."

When her hand found his cheek, Haydn closed his eyes. When his wife's lips touched his, ever so gently, he knew peace and the meaning of contentment. Would that he could stay in this bed, with this woman, forever.

Or mayhap not this bed. Though filled with feathers and not straw, it was not so comfortable as his own in Rymerden. He opened his eyes and she pulled back. Grasping her hand and weaving his fingers through hers, Haydn was content simply to look at her for a time.

"I missed you," he said finally.

"I missed you too. When you rode away that day, I wanted to rail at you. To tell you that I would never, ever, betray you or your family, that you should have realized as much already. To ask if we might find a path forward, together, since I could never be without you again. Instead," she sighed, "I remained silent. But it's what I've known, what I've done, for so long."

"I know, Phillipa. As much as I wish it otherwise, I know. If I could take away every cross word, every strike at the hands of your father, I'd do so. But you must know I welcome your opinion. Your thoughts. If you wish to scream at me, I welcome that too, as long as you love me as I love you."

"I do, of course I do."

He could see the truth of it in her eyes and hoped Phillipa could see the same in his. She smiled then and, quite unexpectedly, jumped from the bed. Too stunned to speak, he sat up and watched as his very naked wife went to her small trunk, pulling out a piece of parchment. Distracted by the way her hips swayed as she sauntered back, he tried to grab her and pull her toward him. But she eluded his grasp, giggling. It wasn't a sound he'd heard from her before.

He liked it.

"No, you must read that first."

Tossing the letter at him, she backed away. Smart woman. Reluctantly, he picked it up and began to read. Haydn's eyes widened as he scanned it. He'd expected a letter to her father and, must admit, was curious what it contained.

Finishing it, he looked up and met her eyes, expectant. Worried even.

"Are you sure?"

She nodded, swallowing. "Aye. I showed it to Holt too. He promised to find me a messenger this eve so it could be sent tomorrow."

A bold move. One he could not be more proud of. "There is just this one part," he said, pointing to a line in the letter. She moved toward him to look at it, realizing too late she'd been well and truly trapped. He pulled her into the bed, leaving the missive, and its repercussions, for later.

# CHAPTER
# TWENTY-NINE

"So good of you to join us," Holt quipped as Haydn and Phillipa joined the others at a table in the hall. The benches easily accommodated them all with room to spare. Reluctant to be separated from her, he sat next to Hamon and pulled his wife down next to him.

In response, she shoved him with her hip, letting Haydn know she didn't appreciate his heavy-handedness. Or maybe she did. Her sideways smile was for him alone.

"Maybe you need more time abovestairs?" Isaac asked across from them.

"They've been up there for the entire day," Holt pointed out, flagging down a serving maid.

"Though we are not complaining," Hamon added. "Not after so many days on the road."

They'd been moving at such a brutal pace. Last eve he'd torn himself away from Phillipa long enough to inform Holt they would be staying here another night. Neither his brother nor the men complained, the town large enough and inn lively enough to hold their interest. Well-rested, they would be on the move again tomorrow.

Once settled, their mugs filled with ale, Holt raised his and looked at his wife. "Phillipa, welcome to the family. You are well and truly a Waryn now, a member of the Brotherhood."

They drank, the mood at their table as jovial as the one in the hall. Fiddlers played as nobles and merchants and travellers drank and sang and laughed. A fight could just as easily break out with nothing but a moment's notice, especially as this particular inn was more of a tavern with room attached. But at present, all was well. And Haydn made no apologies for enjoying peace when it was offered. Turmoil was sure to follow, and when it did, they'd confront it.

"The Brotherhood?"

His men exchanged glances.

It was time.

"It sprang up years ago, even before Edward sacked Berwick and life at the border went from dangerous to downright deadly."

"A term," Holt added, "not of our making."

"You know my Aunt Catrina is the chief of Clan Kerr's sister?" Haydn asked.

"Aye."

"When I came to Kenshire for training," Isaac added, "I'd heard the word bandied about, but it was only when Lord Kenshire, Haydn and Holt's father, knighted me that others began to speak more freely of it."

"It is an alliance between the Waryn family and Clan Kerr."

"I see." Phillipa looked between him and his brother. "But it is common knowledge, is it not? That your families are allied as they're intermarried?"

Holt hid behind his mug. Isaac and Hamon clamped their mouths shut. Haydn leaned in toward his wife, tucked her hair behind one ear, and whispered. "Aye. But 'tis not common knowledge that we support their bid for independence."

Her mouth dropped. He leaned back. There was more to tell her, but this was not the place for it. That his cousin Galien had been with Wallace both at Stirling and Falkirk. That Breac, as Lord Warden, used his influence to ensure safe passage for those, like his family, who also supported Scotland's bid to sever ties with their king. That Rory, an Englishman, had trained with Wallace himself. That Laire, his uncle Reid's daughter, fostered with a prominent English family and risked herself as a spy for Scotland.

"The corridor between Bristol and Brockburg," he said quietly, "the men and women they protect. . . this is what the Brotherhood has come to stand for."

"Our father," Holt said, "was once a reiver. He had strong ties with many reiving families, and they work together to ensure safe crossing."

"Your family. . ." Phillipa was obviously not prepared for the news. He was sorry to have surprised her thus, but she needed to know. "Is allied with. . . reivers?"

"They are not all bad." He shrugged. "Some, we consider kin."

"But. . ." She cleared her throat. "I was told the reivers are thieves and kidnappers."

He didn't deny it, and could not resist laughing at the look on his wife's face. His companions were equally amused.

"You will adore them," he promised her. "At least those who seek shelter at Rymerden or Kenshire when we visit there."

Phillipa seemed skeptical of that.

"So my father and," she lowered her voice, "the king had cause to question your loyalty after all?"

"Undoubtedly," Holt said.

"They did," Haydn agreed.

The four of them watched as a range of emotions crossed his lovely wife's face. From surprise, to doubt. And finally, resignation. She shrugged and picked up her mug. "Then it is good I wrote to Catherine advising her to come north. Haydn said you were successful," she said to Holt, "in finding a trusted messenger with the letter and coin?"

When his wife asked how much she should send so that Catherine could hire safe escort to join them, he told her he would take care of the matter. And he had.

"Aye," his brother said, smiling. "In fact, I believe the messenger to be an extraordinary choice. He is both loyal and strong, more than capable of escorting your sister to Rymerden safely."

"I do not worry she will arrive safely, Holt," he said dryly. "I worry she will arrive uncorrupted."

"Uncorrupted?" Phillipa looked from him to Holt and then back.

"Did I mention handsome?" he said. "In fact, the messenger—"

"Oh no," Phillipa shook her head. "No, Holt."

His brother simply grinned.

She turned to Haydn, her eyes imploring.

"I trust no one else with the task," he explained. "Holt will go with Hamon as we continue to Rymerden. I've already sent word to Hillstone that your maid should rest briefly there and then continue on to join us."

Phillipa gave such a look to his brother that Haydn was sure Holt would behave. Besides, he was no despoiler of innocents. At least, Haydn didn't think he was. And certainly he'd not lay a hand on Phillipa's sister. Phillipa's letter was convincing, but Holt would ensure Catherine understood the need for her to escape her father and the king's clutches.

But they all understood the consequences. Neither Sherfield nor the king would be very pleased.

"If I did not trust and love you as I do, I would cease this plan immediately."

"But you do, and know all will be well. The Brotherhood will protect you, and protect your sister, at all costs." He reached for Phillipa's hand, held it, and squeezed. "I vow it on my life."

# EPILOGUE

"This will be the last inn of our stay. In two days' time, we should be at Rymerden Castle," Haydn said.

Phillipa was grateful for it. Though she knew her husband, and she at times, would be forced to travel again, she was very much looking forward to staying in one place. Amice would arrive, and they could wait for Holt to bring Catherine north.

After that, they did not know.

It seemed likely her father would not seek retribution, even though Haydn had offered to pay a bride price for her sister on behalf of his family. Would he involve the king as well? But Haydn had alleviated any worry she had of bringing unwanted attention to the Waryns by Edward. He assured her, if they were to be on the receiving end of the king's wrath, it would not be because of Catherine.

Indeed, since the night she'd learned of the Brotherhood, Phillipa's eyes continued to be opened. If King Edward truly knew how involved the Earl and Countess of Kenshire and their family were with Wallace—even if they themselves hadn't fought for him—he would likely send an army against them. Enraged at how few of his earls sent men to Annandale and Galloway, he'd already threatened or warned most of them on some level. But for a man who'd been forced to take a wife as a repercussion of his family's decision, and one who had fled with all haste to Bristol to tell his aunt and uncle and cousins of King Edward's renewed focus on them, Haydn seemed remarkably undisturbed about the fallout likely to come because of her sister.

He'd echoed her own thoughts. Come what may, Catherine was best off away from a man who would buy and sell her to the highest bidder. He'd been brutal with Phillipa, but even worse with Catherine. She would be better off in the North. But would the Waryns?

"You'll not recognize me in my own gowns," she said, dismounting. A stableboy met them to take their mounts. She patted Lady on the neck and watched as Isaac and Haydn relieved the packhorse of its supplies.

"Do you not have a squire?" she asked. The thought had occurred to her in the past, though she'd never asked him before.

"I did, but he earned his spurs just this summer. I suppose I will need to find a new one."

"I will take these inside," Isaac said of her trunk and the men's bags.

"Thank you." Haydn walked toward her. "Shall we see if they can draw a hot bath?" he asked, his arms encircling her.

Phillipa laughed. "You bathed in the stream just this morn," she reminded him. They'd stayed the night at an abbey, and though Haydn attempted to get her to come with him to the stream he'd spied as they arrived the night before, she shooed him away. Phillipa might be more outspoken than she'd been when they met. But she wasn't quite ready to be caught naked by an abbess who seemed rather strict. There were few trees to shield the stream located just behind the walls of the abbey.

"I said nothing of bathing," he teased, kissing her in full view of two knights who walked out from the inn.

"You did. You said—"

"That we should get a bath drawn for you."

Phillipa was reluctant to let him go, but the sun had already set, and frankly, she was hungry. "Then perhaps we should eat and do just that," she said just as one of the same men who'd just walked out left his companion to make his way back, as if to talk to her and Haydn. Though her husband had his back to him, Phillipa could see the man's expression quite clearly.

"Haydn." She pushed on his arm so he turned to see him.

The man had a full beard, and though he wasn't as tall or as broad as Haydn, his expression made her back up a step. Haydn's hand moved immediately to his sword, as it did nearly every time they passed someone on the road.

"I am friend, not foe," the man said. "A friend of the Brotherhood."

Her husband's eyes narrowed though he seemed to be immediately put at ease. "It seems you have me at a disadvantage. Have we met before?"

The man looked at her. "We have. At the Tournament of the North two summers ago you bested me in the joust."

"If I injured you—"

"You did not. My pride, but nothing else." He hesitated. "Could we speak alone for a moment? There is information I believe you will be interested in hearing."

Haydn looked down at Phillipa and then back up to the

stranger, who had still not introduced himself. "She stays with me."

His tone was short, and the man didn't question him. He nodded for them to step toward the wall of the inn, which they did. Lowering his voice, he said, "I suspect you'll hear the same inside. Rumors, from the border."

Haydn stiffened. Apparently that was code for "something bad has happened." As they travelled north, the very air around them seemed heavier. Cooler, perhaps, but as if a weight was present that she'd never noticed in the South.

"Rumors," Haydn repeated, "of what?"

"That Wallace is in England," he said, the man's voice no more than a whisper. Haydn's shoulders dropped, relaxing. He knew of Wallace's presence already from his cousins. "And also. . ." The man looked behind him when the door to the inn opened and closed.

Phillipa moved closer to her husband, sure now that something was amiss.

"Tell me," Haydn said.

The man frowned, looked at Phillipa, and then back to her husband. "They say Galien Kerr was spotted with him."

Haydn groaned.

"And that your cousin has been taken prisoner by the king's men."

Travel back in time to when Lady Sara first learned her son would be forced to marry by the king's command in a bonus chapter. Just email Cecelia at cecelia@ceceliamecca.com and say "Give me my bonus, wench!" Or something of the sort.

# GET A BONUS CHAPTER

Not ready for the story to end?

Go beyond the HEA with a bonus scene by subscribing to updates, as well as a dive into the history of *A Noble Betrayal*, via email.

Subscribe at CeceliaMecca.com/Insider

# ENJOY THIS BOOK?

Reviews are extremely important for any author and an essential way to spread the word about the Order of the Broken Blade.

If you enjoyed this book, I would be extremely grateful if you could leave a short review on either Amazon or Goodreads.

# About the Author

Cecelia Mecca is the author of medieval romance, including the Border Series, and sometimes wishes she could be transported back in time to the days of knights and castles. Although the former English teacher's actual home is in Northeast Pennsylvania where she lives with her husband and two children, her online home can be found at Cecelia-Mecca.com. She would love to hear from you.

- Subscribe to be a CM Insider to receive book news and updates via email.

*Connect with Cecelia on:*

f facebook.com/ceceliamecca

🐦 twitter.com/ceceliamecca

𝓟 pinterest.com/ceceliamecca

g goodreads.com/Cecelia_Mecca

BB bookbub.com/authors/cecelia-mecca

# ALSO BY CECELIA MECCA

**Kingdoms of Meria**

The King's Commander

My Highland Bride

Taken by the Elderman

Her Voyager King

**Time Travel**

Sexy Scot

Scandalous Scot

Falling for the Knight

# CONTEMPORARY ROMANCE

**Boys of Bridgewater**

Overruled by Love

Last Call

Billion Dollar Date

My Foolish Heart

# PARANORMAL ROMANCE

**Bloodwite**

The Vampire's Temptation

The Immortal's Salvation

The Hunter's Affection

The Bloodwite Series Box Set